NICE PEOPLE

"Yosevu, you are dirty aren't you?"

"Oh! why?"

"You have given me VD."

"Nduku listen ... ..."

"I want a refund of my three hundred shillings first."

"For what?"

"See for yourself, my doctor says I have gonorrhoea from you."

"How does he figure it is me?"

"I am going go sue you, Yosevu."

I was not worried by either her threats of suing me or her asking me to refund some three hundred shillings. It was her accusing finger that was particularly irritating.

"But you flirt around with your *mzungu* lover, don't you?" I began a subject she was loathe to discuss.

"White men have no VD."

"What are you talking about?"

"Mr. Brown is nice, he does not go with prostitutes."

"How would you know when VD is white or black?"

WAMUGUNDA GETERIA

NICE PEOPLE

Published by African Artefacts
P.O. Box 53697,
Nairobi.
Telephone: 224815/211471

First published in 1992.

ISBN: 9966-9865-0-2

Typeset by Joseph Wanene Gichanga

Cover by Paul Kelemba

Printed by General Printers Ltd.,
P.O Box 18001, Homa Bay Road,
Nairobi, Kenya.

for Njeri, Njeru and Julie Miller whose support and personal
friendship made this book possible.

ABOUT THE AUTHOR

Wamugunda Geteria was born in 1945 at Runyenje's and educated at Kangaru and Alliance High schools, Universities of Ibadan, Oxford and the Australian National. He holds a Master of Forestry degree in environmental and developmental economics. His first novel, *Black Gold of Chepkube* was published in 1985.

ACKNOWLEDGEMENTS

This is a work of fiction and except the names of theatrical personalities, all characters are imaginary. The backgrounds are, however, authentic and I wish to express my gratitude to those who so generously contributed to my research. If in adapting their information to the requirements of a novel I have found it necessary to make changes to information offered I take full responsibility. My deepest appreciation goes to:

Professor Japheth Mati of Nairobi.

Professor S.N. Kinoti of KEMRI, Nairobi.

Professor Ciarunji Chesaina of Nairobi University.

Dr Sobbie Mulindi of the University of Nairobi.

Mr. Wangethi Mwangi of Nation Newspapers Limited.

Miss Monica Ngothi, Miss Joice Nteka and Miss Anne Ndegwa.

Mr. Amos Wanene and family of Karura, Kenya.

"Aids cases world-wide now estimated at close to 150,000 will
double this year partly from the widespread and dangerous
belief that nice people are at little risk..."

Dr Jonathan Mann,
World Health Organization,
1988.

AUTHOR'S NOTE

Among the things that made me embark on *Nice people* was this cutting from the *Sidney Morning Herald* sent to me in June, 1987. I reproduce it here 3 years after:

AIDS in Africa: the crisis that became a catastrophe
by Blaine Harden

NAIROBI,Sunday: AIDS has infected up to a quarter of the population of some cities in central and eastern Africa, where it is now regarded as an unprecedented catastrophe.

The fatal disease is viewed as a particularly severe threat to Africa, the world's poorest continent, because it appears to have spread among its limited pool of professional and technical elite.

Health authorities in Africa and observers elsewhere say the AIDS epidemic could, in a sense, decapitate some African countries.

The growing epidemic, these authorities agree, aggravates an already severe shortage of skilled people and raises the prospect of economic, political and social disorder.

AIDS has hit Africa harder than any other region, according to the World Health Organization (WHO). Studies this year show that AIDS is continuing to spread in some cities at what researchers describe as an alarming rate.

"In terms of deaths, the AIDS epidemic in Africa will soon be as serious as the African famine of a couple of years ago", said Mr Jon Tinker director of the Panos Institute, a London based organization that analyses Third World AIDS data.

"But the famine was a relatively short-term problem. AIDS will continue year after year."

Unlike much of the world, where AIDS has spread primarily through homosexual contact, intravenous drug use and blood transfusion, the disease in Africa is spread primarily through heterosexual contact.

Since the epidemic started in Africa in the late 1970s and early 1980s, men and women have contracted the disease in equal numbers.

Researchers agree that Africa's high rate of untreated venereal disease may play an important factor in the spread of AIDS.

Mr Jonathan Mann, director of WHO's special program on AIDS, said that immediate international support for education, blood screening and strengthening the health systems in African countries - where per capita spending on health averages about $US1.75 ($A2.40) a year - can check the spread of the disease.

VIII

PROLOGUE

Mumbi's funeral was well attended. Dr GG had many friends having kept millions, of Nderu people alive or so they believed. He had seen to many of their children's births, circumcised many of their boys and attended to most of their coughs, gonorrhoea, fever and of late helped what he still considered the "slim" disease sufferers.

I dared not look at him for I knew the suffering he must have been going through. The bond between him and Mumbi, I had for years known, was far greater than any I had known between daughter and father. He had loved Mumbi dearly. Mumbi in turn loved her father very much. I was, she had once said, the only one who could rival the love she had for her father, but because I could not reciprocate hers, it had been allowed to wither off. She had left me for Helsinki to get what I would not give her, a decent home and a family.

She had been an extremely special person, very talented in wit, courage and determination. She was also an extremely honest person not possessing the bigotry Mary Nduku had. She was true to her feelings and she never hid what she felt or believed in. This honesty had driven her to a foreign country believing she was being faithful to Captain Blackmann who had fathered her baby boy.

I looked around and saw her mother who stood nonchalantly and not quite in a mourning mood. She saw me and smiled and although it was not a smiling occasion I smiled back then turned my eyes to see Mary Nduku and Eunice Maimba discussing agitatedly. I wondered what had brought such different personalities together then remembered that I had seen many things in life that wove human beings together. Irene stood next to Dr GG no doubt trying to console the old man with whom she now worked. It must have been a great blow, I thought, for Dr GG to receive the news about his daughter's death in faraway Finland.

It was finally my turn to throw the wreath I held onto the casket. I had avoided viewing the body that many had passed by, paying their last respects to Mumbi. As my bouquet landed on the casket, the tears I had so much tried to conceal began pouring. I did not recall when I had cried last, but I let the warm water flow freely. Here lay Mumbi, I thought, Mumbi the loving, honest, nice person who never fought but always gave way to rivals. She had left for Mombasa because of my affair with Mary Nduku, left Canaan Hospice when she thought her new born son was an embarrassment to me, then left the country to take Master Blackmann where he would feel more at home, amongst his people.

Father Guy had delivered over thirty years ago, a sermon that told of Jesus healing a man called Lazarus then declaring that the man had got sick so that people may believe in God's greatness. Did Mumbi die for the same reason? I wondered. Was the God of love that we had been told about so much in Tala High the same God who caused Mumbi's death or the plague that had nearly shattered my medical career. Dr Ding-Singh had believed in the same God, so had Dr Waweru Gichinga. Dr Ding-Singh had managed to escape while Dr Gichinga had not. Was he a discriminating God, I wondered, to let one flee while the other could not. The same who let a saint like Mumbi die while Mary Nduku survived ..... I was utterly confused as I thought of all these things.

I turned back from the casket that contained the remains of Dr GG s daughter and as I walked away, I felt someone holding me by the arm to keep me from failing. Sister Irene, the dutiful nurse had always, I remembered, been on my side whenever cruel events took hold of me. Yes, I acknowledged the fact that God had also made saints like Irene to keep the sick and the troubled, comfortable. I looked at her and knew that if I really needed some one to take care of me, she would do it willingly.

UNIVERSITY OF IBADAN

Days at the University College were wonderful. The fun we got poring through medical books, with great ambitions of becoming a real special people after graduation, some type of demi-gods curing the many things afflicting human beings. We were supposed to be superior to the veterinarians who treated dogs, cats and horses. As for us we were to treat the superior race — the *homo sapiens* — the greatest of all living creatures. Tuberculosis, malaria, gonorrhoea, syphilis, so many things that man was suffering from these days. Were we really not godsend?

Then one of us was terminated from the University College which we knew simply as UCI. He allegedly stole Dr Martin's heart specimen, which had been circulated around the whole class and he, was believed to be the last to handle it. It had disappeared. The following Monday morning, Adenkule came to class with cooked bits and pieces of meat. He boasted of having cooked the heart. Dr Martin went mad. He called him all sorts of names and Adenkule merely smiled at him, making him even madder.

Then I got down with malaria, the very curse I ironically hoped I, was too strong for. Our final exams, were in a week's time and I knew I was outsmarted by the Almighty, this time. My head boiled and the back felt like it had one dozen lilliputian needles. I writhed in agony and Adenkule came to see me in the dispensary bed at the Jaja Clinic.

"Man you don die of malaria" he quipped in pidgin English. "If doctor Martin had not recommended my discontinuation, I could have cured you, you know." Then Dr William Boyd, a six foot eccentric Englishman walked into the room, ordered me to open my mouth and roughly slid in the clinical thermometer into my mouth. I felt really bad.

Having survived, five rotten years in God forsaken Nigeria with a Biafran war waging all around us, here I was reduced into a helpless mass of flesh.

"You sure are in bad shape," the unorthodox doctor declared after a casual glance at the thermometer with disbelief. He scribbled a few things in my record sheet, then left.

After he was safely out of the sick bay, Adenkule took the record, then after studying it carefully, declared me as dying. I had clocked 104 degrees Fahrenheit. I will not forget that day. My head continued to quake. I tossed in bed, ate nothing, felt dizzy, then passed. I lost consciousness.

The priest must have woken me up. Before me stood a man in white cassock asking me if I needed some time with the Lord.

"No, go away. You only come here when our heads are too foggy to argue with you. Let your God come when we are healthy," I damned.

"What impertinence young man? Are you sure you do not need God's mercy at this hour?"

"On the contrary, I demand of him to cure me if he made me unwell," I answered. "I have done no wrong, if anything I have sacrificed my whole five years to clean his mess of sickness on earth and this is what he rewards me with."

I think it must have been in the Ibadan Dispensary bed, at that very moment, when something snapped in me. I could no longer believe in a God of mercy, love and goodness. What about the millions of beggars, prostitutes, blind-men, cripples and others down-trodden in society? The priests considered all these as God's people. And why the millions spent in pharmaceutical laboratories to cure a disease one day, only to recur again on another day.

Adenkule did not finish his medicine and surgery course. Professor Kola Dambo had submitted his name to the senate for termination.

Before getting our degrees, we had each to sign and affirm the ominous document which Professor Dambo had read for us all:

"I, Joseph Munguti, solemnly pledge myself to consecrate myself to the service of humanity. The Health of my patients will be my first consideration. I will respect the secrets which are confided in me. I will maintain the utmost respect for human life from the time of conception, even under threat, I will not use my medical knowledge contrary to the laws of humanity."
Signed Joseph Munguti,
M.B., Ch.B. (University of Ibadan).

The following day I boarded a Nigerian Airways 8-Seat-Cessna from Ibadan to Lagos. Then at exactly 7.00 p.m., Lagos time, I was in a Pan Am Boeing 707, bound for sweet home Kenya, to start my career. I was now a doctor.

* * *

The plane touched down in Nairobi at 8.00 a.m., that Friday, the next morning the 28th June, 1974. My brother Musembi, took me from Nairobi Airport and drove straight to Tala, my home town. There was jubilation all over the village. Everyone knew that their doctor had arrived. Little did they know that I still had to work as an intern at Kenya Central Hospital (KCH) before looking after them independently. Quite the same, their doctor had arrived.

"Joseph, could you come over here?" my mother called from her room.

"Yes, mother."

"You must go and see your grandfather. He said that he will not take anyone's medicine except yours."

"Oh mum, but why?"

"He believes that the doctors at Machakos have been giving him diluted medicine so that he continues to pay more medical bills."

"Is that possible mama?"

"Well, Kenya is not what you left it, the policemen pray for more criminals so that more bribes are generated, the magistrates want cells to be full, so do the prison warders. We also hear that lawyers are also abetting crime, so they can earn more," she answered. "And you doctors want more gonorrhoea, syphilis and herpes so as to get more work and therefore more money so they say."

"How does my grandfather see me then, if that is his view of the fabric of society?"

"The other day it is said that our resident magistrate took five thousand shillings from a man, then sentenced him to death reasoning that the guy would be too far to tell of their deal."

Mother had not changed. She had been part of Tala gossip for many years and apparently never got drained off the little town's current news. At Tala you needn't mass media to circulate news. Word of mouth did it — and more often than not — exaggerated.

My father, Alex Kilonzo, had seen the worst of times trying to raise a family of fifteen — six sons and seven daughters for whom he sacrificed all the little he had, mainly educating the children. Now pride was evident on his glowing face as he watched me put on the white coat and dangle the stethoscope across my chest. It made him feel that he now had reached the pinnacle of his turbulent life.

We had travelled from Tala that chilly morning of July. The *Matatu* was overcrowded as usual but I did not feel the discomfort having promised myself that was the last *Matatu* journey I was ever going to make. Although the old man did not tell me as much, I was not expected to return to Tala again without my own car or motor-cycle.

* * *

Professor Sylvester Oluoch examined my papers from University of Ibadan, then smiled.
"So Dambo is already a Vice-Chancellor?" the Professor asked.
"Yes, actually since last year. Do you know him?" I enquired.
"We taught together at Makerere in 1965. He went home when the Biafran war broke out," said the Professor.
My father was watching us as he always did whenever he took me to school. Although I was now a grown up man, at twenty-eight years old, he still considered me a care-needing juvenile and even helped me into the white coat that emblematized

medical practitioners. He shook my hand, reminded me not to forget home, whatever I did in the big City.

"I will not forget, dad. I'll be seeing you very soon," I candidly assured him after which he left.

"Have you thought of what you would like to do young man?" Professor Oluoch probed.

"No Professor. I might go into neuro-surgery, but for the time being, I want to remain a general practitioner."

"We have a neuro-surgery case in our hands in Ward Twenty and I think you could start there. The officer in-charge is Dr Waweru Gichinga to whom you will be assigned. You will see it in Wing C," he added, showing me the way out.

"Joseph Munguti *Mwana wa* Kilonzo, M.B., Ch.B., you are going to become the greatest neuro-surgeon this country has seen!" I silently promised myself. Alone, I briskly walked towards Wing C and Ward Twenty, humming to the tune of "My Boy Lollipop."

The bespectacled Dr Gichinga, six foot two, a bit too huge for a Kikuyu, talked with a bit of a stammer. I figured he was in his early forties.

"So you are mm ... my ... new intern are you?" he inquired. "And you have been trained in the University College of Ibadan? ... I hope they did not give you the damned Hippocratic oath," he continued, making me rather nervous.

"They did of course doctor," I answered completely taken aback by the heresy I was hearing from Dr Gichinga. "Don't they give it over here?"

"I read a story of a hangman, young man, who before putting the noose round the condemned men, told them that while he could not rehabilitate them, nor repress their murderous tendencies through the hanging he was about to perform, his children's source of bread, required that he hangs the men, to which the condemned always said, "What the hell are you wasting Hell's time for, hang us and kiss our arses."

"Dr Gichinga, this is a hospital, not a penitentiary?"

"No Sir. This is a prison for all those damned fellows who call themselves medics. They put you here and your conscience, your brains, your power of reason, is switched off. At times, I wish automatons and computers should now take over. Mark my word, you will live to regret the day you entered Ward Twenty."

I was at a loss why Dr Gichinga was so quick in admonishing me with regards to Ward Twenty. I was to find out sooner.

He took me on a guided tour round the Ward, first to his office, then to the Nurses' room, where I met a lovely twenty-year old woman clad in blue.

"This is Sister Irene."

"Good morning," I said

"Morning doctor."

"He is not a doctor yet ," Dr Gichinga corrected, to my embarrassment. He loved to establish this when distancing interns from his experienced types. We then proceeded to see the patients.

"This is Njogu. Njogu is a meningitis case. And that is Opap recovering from a paralysis occasioned by a mild bout of polio. A patient died here last week," he said, pointing to an empty bed. "However, had we had our way, he could not have died."

"What about it doctor?" I asked more amused by this man's eccentricity.

"You will see in a minute," he said, while leading me to a curtained bed at the end of Ward Twenty.

Gilbert was strapped around the life machine. He was the most famous patient at KCH for the past twenty-two months. A road accident had paralysed the whole of his body except the brain, heart and lungs. He fed through his nostrils, breathed with lungs but could not eat solid food. A respiratory and drip machine kept him going and though not speaking, his sparkling eyes were full of life. He could move his head side-ways about a total of 120 degrees, roll his eyes, but that was the only independent movement he was capable of. The rest of him was immobile. For twenty-two months Gilbert lay in Ward Twenty from which he had no escape except by the hand of providence.

"What are your views on euthanasia?" Dr Gichinga started, 'he conversation.

"Euthanasia?"

"Yes, euthanasia, mercy killing?"

"I've never heard of it," I lied, not liking to discuss the subject within the patients' earshot.

"Professor Dambo never talked to you about medical ethics?" He asked.

"He lectured to us about abortions, test tube babies, but never once talked about killing," I lied further.

"Well, Gilbert here wants to die, you can see him angry and mad whenever we come to administer to him. His eyes are always imploring me to save him from the helplessness he must be feeling. But no one dares accept his plea. Some of these are very difficult decisions when we have sworn not to take human life." the Professor resignedly said.

"But have we not sworn not to prolong suffering either?"

"Yeah but what can one do?" he said, helplessly.

The Netherlands were accepting realities on these things and I knew we belonged to different camps. I hoped, however, Kenya Central would awake to the realities, sometime.

This was my introduction to the imprisonment the officer in-charge had referred to. Adherence to rules that are better ignored. I learnt from Gichinga how eleven other patients had so far died, due to lack of the life support system which was hopelessly and exclusively employed on Gilbert. Every nurse and intern dreaded his or her night in Ward Twenty. The Dean had made it quite clear, that anyone under whose care Gilbert died, would be disqualified from medical practice. Gilbert had become the dreaded heel of Achilles for all doctors passing through KCH. He was the determinant factor to ones qualifying for a medical professional practice and was therefore held with both awe and hate.

For the next one week I worked under Dr Gichinga. At first I had found him a bit of an eccentric. I, however, begun to understand him as the days went by. From euthanasia he argued on corruption as an inevitable ingredient in societies such as ours struggling with a capitalism it had; imposed upon it, by the imperialists.

"If you are among thieves, robbers and dishonest men, how could you survive with your honesty?" he once asked me.

"No idea," I answered candidly.

"You see this hospital expects us to be honest with drugs while the Supreme Tender Board has been dishonest in its acquisition methods."

"Oh!"

"They are paying us peanuts while expatriate doctors are housed and paid three times the Kenyan doctor's pay. Expatriates use the government cars that we have no access to. These foreigners are allowed three months' vacations while we receive one, yet we are supposed to sweat just as effectively."

The following Sunday Dr Gichinga took me to his village. We drove from KCH in his dilapidated VW which creaked and quacked all the way through Dagoretti Corner, Kawangware, Uthiru where we nearly collided with a Nairobi bound *Matatu*, then the Nairobi-Nakuru road.

"That was my primary school," Dr Gichinga said."At that time, I hoped I would be a millionaire by now, but as you see, I am still struggling like a church-mouse at KCH." I begun wondering what to tell this man for whom everything appeared hopeless. His hospital, all his outlook in life were based on the dark side of existence.

"But how many Kenyans have jobs let alone cars or are medical doctors?" I asked, trying to make him see the other side of the coin.

"They did not sweat for seven years with cadavers, stinking sores, risked contacting tuberculosis, gonorrhoea, not to mention sitting days on end listening to woeful stories by the hopelessly sick."

I would have told him of the others who live with ditch-diggers, pimps, prostitutes, dope-peddlers or the warders who suffer with prisoners. I would have told him of the policemen whose life primarily entail rubbing shoulders with the underprivileged. Those who patrol stinking streets and whose most eventful life involved the underdogs of society, but I was wiser.

In twenty minutes we reached Sigona Club where golf was played exclusively by the Nairobi rich. On reaching a Mobil petrol station we turned left into Muguga and onwards to a town called Nderu. We stopped at a wooden house in the middle of the amphitheatre-like market place, the main door of which had these words boldly written:

NDERU CLINIC
Dr. WAWERU GICHINGA
M.B., Ch.B. (Mak.)

I looked at him in disbelief. So this hospital-mouse, owned a clinic.

"This will earn you pocket money young man. That is if you choose to co-operate with me ... the government has decided that clinical officers should not man clinics but qualified medical doctors must ... eh ... You are virtually qualified and the old man will back you on the practice. You can earn double your intern allowance if you treated all the VDs of Nderu."

We strode into the clinic, where a sixty-year old man clad in a medical white over-coat and a stethoscope, sleepily sat on a wooden chair.

"Good morning Dr Gichua," Dr Gichinga begun. "This is Dr Munguti who will be working with you."

"Morning doctor," I shook his emaciated hand, taking in an extensive alcohol breath, that nearly intoxicated me instantly.

"*Wi museo*," Dr Gichua begun peering at me the way my old man used to whenever he searched my mind. He smiled and appeared to like me instantly and I could not help being drawn towards him. Other than his drunken state he looked very much like my old man; lean, sharp eyes, pleasant but with a stern look that appeared to tell of his authoritative and stubborn nature when a situation called for it.

"We shall move this town together, this time," he added making me rather perplexed at what this meant. I elected not to inquire into the secrets of Nderu but somehow felt that there was a lot in store, in the clinic, for me.

Dr Gichinga had decided that I would spend five days a week on night duty so as to earn an equivalent time in the Nderu clinic. This appeared a wonderful arrangement because while at Nderu I would earn one hundred shillings per day. He had argued that since the hospital paid me two thousands out of which taxes and the messing fees were deducted, leaving me with what worked to only fifty shillings a day, the one hundred, untaxed, left me double richer than at the KCH. I fully concurred with this, besides life at Nderu where they would not look down upon me as an intern, was quite exhilarating. In fact whenever I left KCH for Nderu my heart pounded with the excitement of one leaving hell for the other place, up with the angels.

* * *

Around eight o'clock, one evening there was a knock at my office door. I walked to the door and opened it and there was Irene, the nurse.

"Yes, Sister Irene," I called out, wondering why she was not in her blue uniform.

"May I come in?" she asked on the instant, walked in, closed the door behind her. She sat on the only seat in my office. I looked at her askance.

"May I call you Joseph sir?" she begun, "Or must I always address you as Dr what-is-his-name? By the way call me Irene."

Although apprehensive, I nearly laughed but she appeared so undecided, whatever was in her mind, that my curiosity gagged me out of my laughter.

"You may call me Munguti," I told her, subtly letting out an old wish for petitioning the registrar of persons with striking "Joseph" (my Jewish label), out of my names.

"Can I talk to you as a doctor?" she begun, with firmness that made me a bit restless.

"Of course you may."

"Am I good looking?"

"Of course you are, why?" I asked spontaneously, wondering what the nurse was up to.

"Why then am I suffering?"

"Are you suffering?"

"Why do I have to sit alone in my room, walk in the streets alone and eat alone. My only joy comes when I am here, washing Gilbert?"

This was a most striking conversation but I made no head or tail of it. Washing Gilbert was supposed to be the most hated duty in Ward Twenty yet here was Irene claiming it was her most rewarding task.

"I wash Gilbert with a lot of joy although I wonder if he appreciates it. He seems the only person in need of me yet he disdainfully looks at me like a zombie not caring and you, you ......" piercingly pointing at me with her left hand finger, she started sobbing intermittently, as tears welled from her eyes.

"What's the matter, Irene," I asked.   I , was quite shy particularly with women. As a doctor however, I managed to marshall courage enough and wore the professional mask.

"I have decided never to take the pill again," she blurted out.

"Well, there are many other alternatives ......" I steeled myself.

"I've decided to quit any form of contraceptive."

"What, the Pope refers to as the natural ......"

"I will not even engage the natural."

"Well then you're talking about a million babies," I suggested.

She then burst into another spurt of sobbing which left me in the awkward position trying to comfort a lady in a pain I could hardly fathom. A million babies could not have been so offending, I thought, then waited for her to volunteer educating me with my faults.

It turned out to be more pathetic than I had possibly imagined. Her mother hated her. Her first lover had made her think that small breasts were unwomanly and she had attributed these to her lack of male company. She often sat in her room alone hoping that a suitor would turn up. None did. Whenever they went out with the few girl-friends she had, all of them would end up accosted by eager partners. Not her.

"What shall I do?" she asked of me.

She had gone to town the previous day determined to catch male company. She had been told that a newly opened night club — The Halian's, was such a beautiful place, for beautiful people, all of single men and women. She wanted to be the nice girl, who does not drink or smoke or visit the so called "places of disrepute". She had only been to a few night spots before. To the 1900 she had gone with John Kimaru her former graduate school lover. She had also been to the Florida with a fellow male-nurse who had lured her into some love-making she was later to detest. The last memory she had of clubs was that of the "Starlight" where too much cigarette smoke had nearly choked her. With trepidation she had queued at the Halian's entrance hall, paid her ten shillings cover charge, then entered the club. There was no empty seat in sight, so she chose the counter high stool, which was quite uncomfortable. She asked for a coke then realising that a beer was more appropriate as she settled, she asked for a Pilsner which she had not taken for some six months.

She proceeded to survey the people who clustered around her, under the dim blue lights. At a corner sat a man with unkempt hair, wearing a leather jacket and seemingly weather-beaten jeans. He sat mute, drinking a Tusker with a care-free forlorn look. It was as if he had no cares in the world as he smoked jetting smoke from his nostrils.

Next to him was a couple who appeared quite agitated in a heated discussion. The man was elderly, perhaps forty-five but the lass was younger than Irene, probably nineteen. She wore a ni-skirt (even if these had gone out of fashion some two years before) She drunk Bulmer's Cider. The middle-aged man gorged some light brownish liquid which must have contained whisky or brandy, Irene thought. He wore a tweed jacket, had an established "Opinion" as beer-bellies were called in those days and on his hands were giant finger-rings that were expensive. He appeared to belong to those rich Nairobi men. The kind who played golf at Sigona or Muthaiga and courted along with them young teenagers to "keep themselves young". All the same, the teenager and her "sugar daddy" appeared to be enjoying themselves thoroughly.

Suddenly, Irene turned to her companions on the counter where a boisterous man drunk, loudly argued with the barman over change.

"Bloody swine, you are every minute, taking people's shillings."

"You are also a swine."

"I will teach you a lesson, you good for nothing barman," he swore then grabbed the barman by the neck, obviously in readiness as if to wring it.

"Please don't," Irene shrieked. "I'll pay the shilling."

"Who asked for your money you *malaya*?" the drunk retorted menacingly turning from the barman to Irene, but his grip still on the barman.

"You dare call me a *malaya*? I am a Registered Nurse!" she shouted defiantly, then felt all the Halian's eyes looking at her. Compunction immediately struck her as the full effect of her disclosure bore upon her. A Registered Nurse, drinking beer at Halian's, all alone. She instantly stood up and fled the Halian's, leaving her untouched drunk Pilsner, behind.

It was a bit chilly and she undecidedly walked along the Tom Mboya Street toward River Road. She crossed Latema Street then thought of entering into Luthuli Avenue. She was about to run towards the Hole-in-the-wall, when she recalled a busy, small, but nice rendezvous called, The Arch, by the Ambassadeur Hotel. Something told her that, that was a Canaan. If Halian's will not welcome Registered Nurses, The Arch surely should.

She asked for a Pilsner as she sat on a strategic corner all alone. She removed her make-up mirror, powdered her nose then sat feeling extremely restless. Her whole body was burning, particularly below her thighs and she moaned inside wondering how the professionals conquered men. Suddenly she begun laughing at the thought that prostitutes were more preferred than decent nice people like herself. Those who never asked to be paid for bed-favours, were clean, unsoiled and decent. What a paradox? Nairobi was crazy, she thought, as she continued to sip her Pilsner.

"May be I should turn into a harlot, after all," she said thinking aloud. As if her call to heavens was being heard, with the corner of her eye, she saw a fairly decent looking fellow approaching her table.

"May I join you?" he even had the audacity, to ask.

"Sure!" she said, a bit more eagerly than allowable then stared at the man.

"What shall I offer you?"

She could have collapsed on realizing the second gaffe of the day. Women in Nairobi didn't just offer strangers beer, rather it was the vice-versa.

"What?" the bank executive asked.

"I thought you wanted something," she recollected herself, not quite sure how to proceed. However, it worked. The man took the seat opposite hers, ordered for a Tusker and a Pilsner for her. They soon engaged in a light-hearted argument as to who would pay for the drinks with Irene insisting on picking the tab for the man's Tusker and he, for her Pilsner. In the process she learnt that the man's name was Leonard and he worked as a chief teller in the Bank of India.

"To cut a long story short," Irene told me in a raised voice, ended up with this six footer who could easily pass for a boxer, .pole-vaulter or something, at Rwathia across the road. "He booked us into this filthy hotel, then set to work on Irene the Nurse you now see here. He was such an animal. He kept re-assuring me that he could add more money."

"Dr Munguti, what type of clay are men made of? I offer myself to a man of my heart and he hurts my feelings because he considered me for sale, me, me ..." She broke into compulsive sobs and I found myself feeling fairly mad with Leonard.

I examined her neck and determined that she had superficial lacerations. I managed her with Iodine and reckoned that she would quickly recover from the scratches. I was not sure, however, whether she would find psychological cure because she had left the hospital while still in some kind of hysteria.

* * *

Irene at twenty-five, stood five feet seven inches which is considered tall for Kenyan women. She was not particularly attractive, especially her face which appeared longer than normal but had extravagantly shapely hips and well-kneaded legs. Her waist began slightly higher than she preferred and her breasts, the other defect she thought, having once been told so by her first suitor, were very small. Socially she was lonely with only a few friends for reasons she could not quite understand.

As we continued to see each other in Ward Twenty, I got to know her better. Her childhood days, schooling and the five years in KCH where on completing a three-years' Registered Nurse course, she pursued a final year in advanced nursing training specialising on theatre duties.

She could not precisely establish how her shyness developed but she knew that she had been brought up a bit too strictly. Her mother had appeared to hate her, for example, taking on the rod every time she did wrong. She remembered one day, for example when as she did her hair to go to church, her mother, disapproved her rather coquettish hair style.

"Irene how many times shall I warn you about hair dressing?" she begun threateningly.

"What have I done wrong mummy," she responded.

In a flash her mother jumped on her, pulled her neck, bending her double and mercilessly re-brushed her hair, cursing her as a good-for-nothing trollop.

20

"You are hurting me,mummy" she screamed. Then her mother started to rain blows on her. Irene was only saved by her father, who happened to come home just then.

Her father was always supportive of her and when she grew up, she came to believe that this support and love for a daughter perhaps earned her, the mother's displeasure. It was as if dad and daughter were enjoined in a battle with an adversary who tormented them both. The more she affronted them, the more their bond galvanised.

When Irene was sixteen, she had brought a boyfriend home. Jameson Orengo belonged to a tribe, — the Luo —, which her mother loathed. She had found them sitting in their living room in South B playing some Jimmy Cliff's records that Irene liked. There was no misconception of the hatred and disapproval with which Naomi, Irene's mother, looked at them, as she entered the room.

"And what do you think you are doing, you lass, sitting down the whole day?" she begun.

"But we have just arrived mummy," Irene protested.

"You have not swept the floor, not peeled potatoes, or done the dishes," her mother continued as if she heard no response.

Then Irene protested that the maid was there for such things and that she deserved some time especially with her visitors.

"Which visitors you lass?" her mother howled, showing her utter disgust at the mention of Chief Opande's son as a visitor to her home.

Orengo a first year law student at the University of Nairobi, had known Irene since she was a child. They had played together often but had all along noted Naomi's dislike of his family which was apparently well to do within Nairobi. His father, Chief Opande, was a much respected business-man in Nairobi. As a councillor, he has assisted in issuance of traditional liquor licenses, allocated plots and settled many domestic and civil disputes for which he is believed to have done for consideration. He drove a Volvo since the time Orengo was in high school. He was one of the first Africans, to own a television set (cars and television sets marked one's station in opulence during the sixties).

They had hoped that Naomi would mellow with time and realize that the new generation of Kikuyus and Luos needed not to live in artificial hatred of each other. But on studying Irene's mother's face on this day, he knew that it was yet, before he was welcome in Naomi's home. He stood to go.

"You will sit down!" Irene ordered Orengo in rage knowing that her mother had to be defied now. She wished her dad was around to defend her. He was away at the Standard Bank where he had worked for thirty years.

Orengo had left and Irene had sworn to teach her mother a lesson some day. She believed that she knew a few of her secrets and she would therefore appropriately pay her with an equal measure — no matter how long it took. She lost him.

After Orengo, she would not bring anyone to their home. And as if mother sought all her Achilles' heels, she had quipped over her lack of friends.

Kamanja was a reserved man, he never shouted or howled as Naomi did. He was in most things the antithesis of his wife who was boisterous, loud, cantankerous and extremely uncompromising. Naomi had four children, three sons now grown up and Irene whom he loved dearly. He was not quite sure about his love for Naomi. She worked for the East African Airways, earned much more than him. She spent half of the week on sales' promotion tours only to come home and complain that things she indicated should be done, had not been done. If done, she hardly gave credit. Recently, he had suspected she had taken on drinking and lovers, although he had not as yet established these wild feelings. All he noticed was that she had become less generous in her love for him and grew more critical at the slightest opinions Kamanja could conceive.

"All your other children are alive, with friends, you are a loser," she said. Irene continued with life alone, friendless and a virgin even beyond the day she left high school at the age of eighteen.

I was the prefect on duty one day during our last year at Tala High School. Father Guy Benedicto (locally referred to as Ventigito Mubea), the Principal, was a highly respected man . He led the mass, preached every Sunday to us and listened not only to the students' confessions but accepted those of the surrounding community. This was for two days a week, Saturdays and Tuesdays, between the hours of five and six at sunset. A real workaholic with remarkable strength. I admired the priest and knew he had some liking for me because I loved his Chemistry subject. I was the only student who had unlimited access to him. Whenever I needed him, I would go to his house, office or reach him even at the vestry. In return for this privilege I traded with him all the information he required about the school. Much later in life I came to realise that Father Benedicto required my association to run Tala High School.

"How was food today?" he would ask for instance and I would tell him candidly, that it had been delicious.

"How was the sermon?"

"Excellent." I would sometimes lie so as not to offend him.

"How is Physics?" he asked me one day and I went on to describe how Tom Saunders could not easily explain Boyle's Law with the lunar capsule which many students did not understand. He took a lot of interest on how the American Peace Corps volunteer was faring and appeared sad that his "English" was complicated. Some students could not tell what "warer" for water and "morocar" for motor—car as Americans pronounce it, were. To this Father Guy laughed uncontrollably.

One day and I can't remember how we came to it, I must have told him that one was not considered man enough in Kamba–land if he was of age and unmarried. One had either be a half-man, impotent or a casanova, all which did not augur well with the tribesmen. The next day during the mass he made a sermon half of which he gave in Kikamba.

"I understand some of you wonder why Father Guy is not married. He is not married to one person but to all the women. Whose wives do you think all these belong?" he challenged.

"To the father!" the congregation answered in an uproar.

"We servants of the Lord were commanded, years ago, not to get attached to one person. We belong to all humanity and this is why all of us including the Pope must be celibates so that we can spread the Word of the Lord"

A few days latter, I had an almost choking experience when I went to Father Guy's office. The Church door was open, but the vestry was locked. Under normal circumstances when Father Guy was inside the church neither the main door, nor the door to the vestry, was locked and I would always walk in. This time I had to knock. When he opened after several knocks, he appeared pale, his hair was ruffled and Mrs. Saunders was sitting on the couch.

"These are the Chemistry books Father," I explained, feeling rather awkward.

"Oh sure, come in and say hello to Mrs. Saunders. She almost fainted at Kennedy's death," Father Guy said, without apparent emotion. I knew Robert Kennedy as the brother of the youthful American President mowed down by a gunman in Dallas sometime back. I however, must confess that I did not know he was popular even to the people in faraway Kenya. And if that be true, then Mrs. Saunders must have been extremely affected. She was dazed. That was then. I was young and that is all I saw. If I was older, perhaps, I would have seen more.

A week later, Father Guy, an Italian, left Tala. We thought he had gone to attend the funeral of the American politician. He was never to return. We hadn't noticed that Mrs. Saunders had left at the same time. But we learned that Tom Saunders nearly committed suicide when he came to grips with the disappearance of his wife. Kambas would have set on a war-path if they lost their wives to other men in similar circumstances.

Mary Nduku was five feet two inches, of light complexion which the Kambas considered beautiful. She didn't have a known father but had learnt from her mother that she was the daughter of an important personality. Mwende, the mother of Nduku, had six children all by different men. But she chose her drones carefully, like a queen bee. She had worked as a cook in Tala High then as a cateress in Nyeri approved school. Her first child, John, was by the village headman who provided for the boy for two years hoping to keep Mwende. She however, did not wish to be a second wife, so she moved on and begot with a school headmaster who was later to become a District officer and then a District Commissioner. Then came Kavilla less than a year later by an army Sergeant Major, who had seen the Second World War in Korea. On his return he was attached to the King's African Rifles, to fight the Mau Mau when he met Mwende at Nyeri Approved School.

Dr John Kimani fathered the fourth and fifth children at the height of the state of emergency. Those were hard times for the family living in Nyeri township where the Mau Mau war had wreaked havoc and as a result food supply became scarce and extremely expensive.

Her choice of Dr Kimani as the temporary man of the house could not have come at a better time. In his position at that time of political upheaval, he managed to provide for the family although he never really intended to marry her. The people of Embu, Meru and Kikuyu extraction had been placed in concentration camps, in an effort to weed out the Mau Mau from the reserves.

By the time the last child Rebecca was born, Nduku was already pursuing high school education in Tala. She had made one decision — that she would not be like her mother — so many husbands and so many "fatherless" children. Whenever the question of her father occurred to her, Nduku would weep deep inside because she felt she had not been brought up as a normal child should.

Mwende was a woman of generous social proportions. Extremely hard working, shrewd and stubborn. There is nothing she did not know about men's habits. She carefully chose her mates and almost with mathematical precision she picked pregnancies. She demanded nothing on maintenance from the children's fathers other than the acceptance that she was a nice person whose only fault was that no man would stand her for more than a week. After that, her irascibility would interfere with a relationship and eject a man out of her life. They came as they went. And the more they left, the more she was determined to prove that she was capable, of raising a decent family, well fed, clothed and educated.

When Nduku reminded me all this, she was herself already a secretary in Nairobi. I had met her in a New Year's dance, at the medical school where an old classmate at Tala had brought her. I had known her as one of Mwende's children over fifteen years before, but had not seen her since then. Steve a clinical psychology lecturer at the Nairobi University, had made her pregnant at eighteen, immediately she had left Tala High School.

I pretended I did not know her as Steve introduced us.

"This is Dr Munguti, Joe this is Mary, we are very close," Steve introduced us.

"No, we are not close, He closed in six years ago and converted me into a mother then departed," Mary said, with a whipping voice. She startled me with the openness with which she qualified Steve's introduction.

"Yosevu, are you sure you don't know me?" she enquired.

As a child, I was known as Yosevu and only those who knew me those two decades ago would use this name. I looked at her, Mwende's little girl, now fully grown up. A full woman. I noticed something decent in her mannerisms if decency meant opening the mouth and eyes not too widely, sipping whatever she was drinking noiselessly, nodding imperiously as she listened and turning the head gracefully only a few degrees when the occasion required.

I gathered that she knew a great deal of the present day me. Whoever had told her of my internship at KCH and "the little hospital" in Nderu Market? I wondered.

In acknowledgement I said, "You are Nduku, the beautiful one of Nyeri Approved School!" I had surely known her when I used to visit my father during the holidays in Nyeri. My father had been transferred to work in Nyeri during the Emergency. He was what the colonial government called a rehabilitation officer who was to preach to the Mau Mau detainees the need to denounce violence and accept the white man's rule.

We lived in the same camp with the Mwende family then and I believe my father was the only V.I.P. who never entered Nduku's mother's den. We were six then, they were six, but with a difference. My mother had a husband while Nduku's had none. I did not know that our social status was the envy of Nduku and that she had become then obsessed with the idea of raising a decent family like ours.

Steve's baby may have been an accident along this path, but she was determined quite the same. She smiled at me, called me rather familiarly and I could not mistake the challenge she was offering. Then suddenly she moved away from my friend Steve, who was now married but was still taking care of John their child.

Then I was to learn that Nduku lived well. She would not dress in locally made clothes or shoes. Her house was exquisitely furnished — all maroon and mahogany, wall to wall carpeted and an appointed kitchen. How she managed called for hard work. Her lover Ian Brown was English and worked for the local Standard Bank as a Loans Manager. She was his secretary and gave exactly what bosses asked for — absolute loyalty.

Ian Brown was thirty four, tall and of straight-jacket upbringing.
His grandfather had left Sheffield, England before World War II,
years ago and gone to South Africa where he managed one of the
original Standard Banks. From South Africa he came to Kenya and
pioneered the Standard Bank of South Africa which was one of the
earliest institutions to conduct banking in Nairobi. This is where
Ian now worked, in the Loans Department. He was rich by
Kenyan standards living in Muthaiga, the Beverly Hills of Nairobi.
He drove a Jaguar, played golf at the Muthaiga and other leading
clubs but his most loved spot in Nairobi was the Club 1900.

Club 1900 was a pick-up place with a difference. It attracted
all, even those who practiced the known Western love-making
deviant practices such as whipping, trio-some encounters, fellatios,
cunningulus, use of vibrators and sodomy. Both male and female
assembled in the Club 1900, mainly to attract the Yens, Dollars,
Deutsche Marks and Sterling pounds.

It was Mary Nduku's large breasts that first attracted Ian. He
would ogle at her as she took his dictation. She instantly became
aware of this attraction and began to wear blouses with a bigger V
than previously. She noticed that Ian's eyes dilated even further
and could hardly keep his eyes off her bosom. He called her in for
more dictation than on previous days. She came to learn that the
Englishmen admired large-size breasted women and it was no
wonder that the pages of such magazines as the Playboy, Pent-
house and Men-only, were full of these type of nude pictures.

Mary hadn't said anything on Ian Brown when we met. We
had danced her large breasts pressing on me, with an unmistaken

sign of invitation. I, having had no girlfriend for most of the years we were in Ibadan, welcomed the challenge of a beautiful Kamba girl. She had given me a number which I followed a few days after to gain a long waited date at the Serena Hotel.

When the day came, I drunk a White Cap and she took a Martini for which I paid a fortune — nineteen shillings.

I paid this money and almost swore never to visit Serena again. She had a 304, with which she drove me to Nderu. We spent a night in the local boarding house, a wonderful night. So different from the encounters with Ibadan two-Naira' prostitutes.

Mary and I continued to see each other and then she confided in me bits and pieces about Ian Brown.

One day she carelessly left her hand-bag at the clinic and I curiously opened an envelope that she must have loved carrying around. It had pictures that could have landed her in jail for pornography. In one such picture was a black woman in a sodomy pause. In the other was a white man apparently making love with an African female. Something was not quite right with the second picture. I could have puked.

She found me in such a rage, I could have killed her. She, however, explained that she was not Brown's lover but that Opundo his cook was. Nduku's place in his life was that of a screen for his homosexual tendencies. For this, he bought her a house, a car and allowed her unlimited bank loans. She assured me that it was I, Dr Joseph Munguti who mattered in her life, a claim, I could neither accept nor stay long enough to validate.

Someone had to rescue me from the clutches of Nduku. She was a determined woman, who never gave up easily. A lot of women in Nairobi, she made me understand, had a chain of lovers from whom they eked millions. Her colleague secretaries ran three or four business executives as boy friends at any one time and that in fact, one of her friends had three men meet her maternity expenses at one time, all believing they had sired a single son. She was not of this type, she beseeched me.

She was a nice girl who did not have as many lovers. Ian Brown actually never made love to her but paid for the make-believe in the Standard Bank, Muthaiga and Sigona Club that he was a nice, rich, celibate and not the homosexual he was. I was sorry for Nduku because, I disapproved the role she played in Brown's life no matter what the cause was. I could not at the time, however, tell whether I was jealous of the rich Englishman or simply expressing myself as one who loathed homosexuals.

Halima had only one alternative. All the kids were going to die. Two of them lay helplessly on a makeshift couch of her tiny room that no longer welcomed lovers. Mulishi the girl, was the weakest followed by Makenya who was two. Makobo, other than for the diarrhoea that had attacked him, could be spared. He could hardly stand but could speak. He was four and a half, a brilliant kid that if this famine spared, might support her in her old age. Nora had gone to look for food the previous day and had not returned.

Nora knew that coming home empty handed, would not be pleasant. Her not returning, indicated that she was still searching or had decided to fend for herself. At five and a half this was quite understandable as this is the age when self-preservation dominates children's minds. As for her twins aged seven, Halima no longer cared where they went, since the two appeared to hate and fear her. Other children had fled to Mwanza where her parents lived and people still survived on carcasses.

Halima recalled the sixth day of lack of food in her house. Bukoba, as almost the rest of Tanzania was literally starved. The neighbouring countries were only slightly better. Uganda and Kenya were also experiencing difficulties. The rains had failed for three consecutive years. Two days earlier, she had made weak porridge out of tappings of flour sacks. These were not available from the shop any more. People did not throw away food any more! Nor did they want their smiles. The shopkeeper in the neighbourhood was particularly hostile when she had suggested a credit for flour. It was as if he had no strength or wish to have her present herself in lieu of the three shillings worth of flour. How miserable a world could be?

Halima re-lived her painful experience to me with a lot of difficulties. In frustration, she had killed the youngest child. A mercy killing? She was tried and acquitted of infanticide, after all the facts had been known, but she never quite recovered from fear of want or hunger. This is why she ate and drank hard at every opportunity in an effort to ward off "famine", she explained to me. It was all in her mind, a figment of imagination.

"Doctor, how can you after what I have gone through, encourage me to have another baby?" she asked me with apparent venom. "You men fecundate nice people, walk off straight and then deny us, the sufferers, any say about our suffering."

I had to accept that she was right although Darwin in his survival of the fittest theory, could have had something to say about the forces that work on mothers, fathers and others to allow babies be born even by imbeciles and the lunatic.

I promised to help, after which she left.

* * *

A few car owners did like their lot, the twi-light girls. They would be seen around the regular spots such as Mama Ngina Street, Standard, Post Office and City Hall Way which by 11.00 p.m., every night, were almost deserted. Driving at say 10 kilometres an hour, the drivers' faces would be clearly visible as they peeped into the dark alleys for the night girls. Occasionally the Police would disrupt the nests, but from the lamp-posts in the corners of streets, it was easy to pretend the girls were not up to that age-old crime of loitering with immoral intent.

Halima was pregnant and she well knew how much she was to blame herself for it. She certainly was not going to have a seventh, yet as the days milled by, she found herself becoming more desperate. She had to terminate the pregnancy at whatever the cost. Around the ninth week, she had gulped six Malariaquine tablets hoping they would do the trick. Instead they made her crazy for a whole day, but left her foetus intact. Still determined, she had on a another week drunk contents of Colman's Azure Blue, the dye used for bluing clothes but again this too, did not work.

She recollected and constantly practiced all the do-not-dos about a pregnancy although she was aware of other risks she exposed herself to. She would smoke, drink heavier than before, get as many sexual partners as possible while she continued to hunt for an abortionist.

She had been informed of the possibility of getting a proper abortion from KCH at the cost of around, two thousand shillings, but how to go about it was quite problematic. The law in Kenya was very stringent in regard to abortions and both the doctor and their clients risked several years in jail. She had confided in Josephine, her street companion on her problem as she narrated about her five starving kids in Bukoba who had been left behind with a sister. She had even engaged in collection of two shillings at Pumwani for each quickie with a hope of making enough money to sustain her family. At Pumwani they would sit whole days, from about nine o'clock in the morning outside the small mud-houses which had apparently been built for prostitution. Men of all shapes, sizes and description would walk through the narrow alleys of *Majengo* and the women would grin to attract them.

She recalled how they would smile and wink at the passing males. Some would curse them when they made as if to hold them. The indignities they suffered, but bravely swallowed as they attracted the Pumwani short-timers! Catching a client was a hope. An even bigger problem was getting one to pay for the services. With some, one asked for the cash before climbing on the bed with him. With some she gambled hoping that the fee would be paid afterwards.

The act ended at an ejaculation irrespective of how long one stayed on top of one or how rough they were. And they were even rougher, Halima noticed, whenever made to pay in advance, but for some, this haste brought faster ejaculations and consequently was preferred, especially in the mornings, when one was fresher. Some had not bothered to remove shoes. Others would mount even with trousers on, while a few insisted on a bestial position.

There were also some drunks who would not ejaculate but would go on seemingly forever and this would begin to hurt. If she would demand that they should finish, they would do so angrily and demand their two shillings. If she refused as she would at times, the risks of having her nose broken could be a matter of course. Then there were the arduous middle of the month days, from about the twentieth day of the month, when business slackened. Fewer people showed up at *Majengo* and those who did, were less than generous. They would ask for sex at a discount or at times fifty cents in all!

Halima had stayed in Pumwani, *Majengo* for a year before resigning from the business and joining the lamp-post girls who roamed the corners of down town Nairobi main streets.

I learned all this from her visits to KCH, as she struggled to convince me to procure an abortion. But then Josephine introduced her to Dr Gichinga who accepted five hundred shillings. He administered anti-candida tablets and ointments for her intimate parts but did not rid her of the pregnancy.

"Why must I risk a jail term over a waste paper material. For all I know the baby inside her is as good as deformed!" he told me one day. "You should now be able to handle safer 'Defoetasions'." He preferred this term he had coined, to the obnoxious one, "abortion". As a rule Gichinga, never operated on abortions after eight weeks of pregnancy.

She continued to visit Ward 20 where Dr Gichinga had now set up a consultancy (albeit illegally) and leave with medicines and ointments being assured that her pregnancy would terminate.

Halima had come to Ward 20 during her thirteenth week. The tummy was beginning to show by now. She told me of how desperate she had become. She had started dancing in the Starlight and even picking fights with men in the hope that they would induce abortion or merely kick her baby out.

The booze, cigarettes and fees for the night-clubs were now draining her savings while the hazard continued to grow in her. Dr Gichinga now felt harassed by her. He had warned her not to visit KCH again. And that if she pestered him again, he had threatened, he would have her picked for illegal residence in Kenya.

* * *

Dr Gichinga was in his usual grumpy moods. He sat on the examination bed, lifted his long legs and placed them before us on the waiting table eyeing Irene and I who stood at attention listening to his tirade. I was getting used to his moods by now.

"There is something dangerously wrong with laws that have no sense for social values .." Dr Gichinga begun.

"Like which?" Irene asked.

"Consider this crap against procurement of abortion, for instance. They have outlived their purpose in an overpopulated planet."

"But they still have some societal values," I objected.

"Dr Munguti, the day God commanded Mr. Adam and Eve to go into the world and multiply are long gone. At the time it was necessary for all conceptions to bear fruit."

"How about Darwin's postulation of the survival of the fittest theory?" I thought I should be scientific rather than mythical.

"Even then," Dr Gichinga explained. "It was imperative that for the survival of the fittest, the foetal material be assured development without interference, natural or otherwise. In the development of the uterus, this was guaranteed. In all mammals the uterus is a highly complex organ like a very complex safe which locks up the foetus once conception is made and ensures that whatever is inside comes out at considerable risk to the safe-keeper."

"Oh yeah?" I wondered.

"We of course have things like spontaneous abortions, induced or otherwise which ensure that when things go wrong in the development of the foetus, it is ejected," Dr Gichinga continued. "This is basic medicine I know, but it is important sometimes to revise our notes. Now we have the Pope who says that the foetus is sacrosanct and no sufficient reason can be advanced for its

36

removal, whether the mothers are children, imbeciles, rape victims, whatsoever," he said raising his hands in the air as if in resignation.

"Britain has now accepted mothers' health considerations," I suggested. "And some states of America have even gone further and accepted that maternal consent for births is necessary. I think Japan has pregnancies, abortions, motherhood and birth events as options available for everyone."

"In Kenya the option appears to be for those who can afford some three thousand shillings," Irene suggested.

"Incidentally, why is it so expensive?" I wondered.

"It is a risky business because the law outlaws it. Secondly since it is done under clandestine conditions, this makes it intrinsically expensive. One has to conduct anaesthesia, blood transfusions and related surgical tasks in a non-conventional arena," Dr Gichinga said raising his voice.

It was obvious that this was one of those social problems that had no ready-made solutions. The law prescribed one thing but the social dictates were left to see to its applicability.

"Besides the health of the mother, that of the child and the social welfare of existing children, are considerations Britain is making," Dr Gichinga continued.

"Abortion can be an effective method of population control better than contraceptives," Irene added.

"No wonder such countries as Japan, Sweden and Finland are now experiencing negative population growth," I said.

"And women have to be encouraged to bear children," Irene finished for me, putting the debate to an end. But only then.

* * *

I discussed Halima's case with Dr Gichua who burst out laughing hysterically. The old man stood up in uncontrollable fits, firmed himself against the examination bed. He contorted with gasps of laughter until tear-drops rolled down his cheeks.

"You mean you modern-day doctors cannot cope with a thing that even old village women have dealt with for millenniums?" he asked. "We have removed foetal material many a time with such simple tools. Bring the lady to the all cure Nderu Clinic," he directed.

Godfrey Maimba was fifty. His wife was seven years younger. They lived in the posh Redhill area, where the Nairobi businessmen and other executives lived on five acre pieces of land. They had a choice and well appointed house, all burglar-proof with the latest electronic devices. And despite the electronics, a Securicor guard watched over the house on a 24 hourly vigil.

Eunice Maimba worked as the most senior secretary—infact a personal assistant—at the University of Nairobi, a job that despite their wealth, she treasured to keep her active and useful. Maimba was a chief executive of one of the largest banks in the country.

He was a model husband, or was he? He neither drank alcohol, smoked nor flirted with Nairobi prostitutes. He was extremely devoted to a wife whom, for twenty years he drove from their residence to work, promptly collected and drove back home. At home they would watch television together, dine together, then dutifully retire to their bedroom at 10.00 p.m. Their life when in Nairobi was the envy of many among their friends and neighbours.

* * *

They brought her to Nairobi Hospital at twelve o'clock. She bled profusely from a laceration on the fore-head, just above the left eye.

At first I could not decipher her incoherence in Kikuyu but the repeated nature of the words brought out what she was saying.

"Give me more. Father of Njeri, more,. . ." she shrieked to everyone's amazement.

Maimba was all embarrassment as his deranged wife continued with her litany for more of whatever she was having. It was only when the whole incident unfolded that we were able to make sense of what Eunice persistently requested her husband to provide.

It was apparent that Maimba had no time to dress-up. He was in expensive silk pajamas under a woolen night gown. His hair was raffled and he explained that he had to rush "the Mrs" to the Hospital as she was bleeding and delirious.

"Not working today," he explained."My hypertension started again and I took the morning off. This seems to have affected the Mrs," he added.

"More, more!" Eunice continued, heaving her bleeding head dangerously.

I had come to visit Prof. Onguti a consultant at the Nairobi Hospital which is across the street from KCH. When Mrs. Maimba was brought in, the professor was seeing me off at the ambulatory.

"You must hold the lady's head firmly if you hope to cure her physiologically," The Professor admonished a nurse. The nurse then held her by the head as if they were in a combat as I held firm her hands then we led her to the examination bed to which she had to be strapped for fear of doing damage to herself. Prof. Onguti decided on sedating her which was done before proceeding with the examination of her forehead, whose cut was deep and required 'quite a bit of stitching. Prof. Onguti was reputed in maxilla-facial surgery as he had perfected the art in fifteen years.

His only problem was constant complaints about patients that could not keep still even under heavy doses of local anaesthetic. The nurse helped him with the oxygen while I handed him the surgical instruments, cutting the thread as he stitched. Within 12 minutes Mrs. Maimba's wound was all sown up and she could be released but for anaesthesia. Her mind was however still focused on the material she was insatiably crying for from "Baba Njeri", the intimate name she used to address her husband.

"Well, as for The Ambulatory, the patient was done for the day. The rest was to be handled by the in—patient department."

Prof. Onguti announced waving his hands in the air, after which she was portered on the stretcher to Maya Carberry Ward.

It was during her stay in the ward that the strange story about Mrs. Maimba's strange ailment unfolded.

The previous day Maimba had announced he would be going to Mombasa for the Federation of Kenya Employers' annual Conference. He had the chauffeur collect him in the company Mercedes car at 7.00 a.m. with a suit-case full of personal effects including razors, toothbrushes, combs, socks, underwear, vests, shirts and three safari-suits to last him a week. As usual Mrs. Maimba had personally supervised the packing of the clothes that she in person put in the boot of the car. Maimba had left at seven o'clock in the morning promising to ring on arriving in Mombasa and hoping to return after five days.

Mrs. Maimba had left at 7.30 a.m. in their smaller car, a BMW and gone to her place of work at the University. On reaching her office she found a note from the Vice-Chancellor that he too had gone to Mombasa for the same conference. She already knew that he would be away anyway.

The Vice-Chancellor's secretary found herself without typing or dictation to take and decided to dash home to collect the knitting she was doing for her expected grandchild. She drove back home at ten arriving at their Redhill home at half past ten.

The watchman opened the door for her as he normally did and she entered the house through the kitchen. She darted across the living room into their bedroom, which had not been locked. At first she thought she was dreaming for she had never seen such an act even in movies. She simply couldn't believe what she saw. It couldn't be her bedroom. On focusing closely she realised that it was her husband with their maid Mwanaisha. She was shocked. Could it be true? She hoped against hope.

"Baba Njeri!" she started, unbelieving. It was when she screamed that Godfrey Maimba realized that the maid and himself had extra company in the form of Mrs. Maimba.

Mrs. Maimba never quite recovered from the hallucinations. It was then decided to consult a leading psycho-medic outside the hospital to unravel the strange ailment.

A leading clinical psychologist, Dr Daniel Ndetei established that she had suffered a sudden delirium tremens — a severe psychotic condition the moment she saw her husband in bed with her house-girl. She had believed it was herself who was shrieking and enjoying the bliss. It was like old times when she was young and Godfrey was then madly in love with her giving her absolute bliss, hence her cries. She had a calenture of the brain, a black-out then banged herself on a porcelain flower-vase cutting her forehead badly with the knife-edged part of the ornament.

They had strapped her on a chair to try and control her, after which Dr Ndetei slowly began to uncover the screen behind Mrs. Maimba's sudden dementation.

She had never even dreamt of her husband sleeping with another woman all those twenty years she lived with him. To her, only her body could grace her husband as there was no other person either capable or with an opportunity for sleeping with her husband. She herself had only had one sexual encounter before Godfrey many years ago and even then under peer pressure. She had visited the men's hall of residence at the University of Nairobi and had it, no emotions, no pleasures, as bad bad can be.

It was not possible to get much out of Mrs. Maimba at first as she had continued with her delusions, raving until the early hours of the night. Dr Ndetei had therefore decided to sedate her after which she was laid in the hospital bed under the vigil of her bewildered husband.

She woke up at ten o'clock and to everyone's amazement started where she had left. It was at this time that Dr Ndetei thought the problem was far more serious than the hospital had earlier thought.

Maya Carberry walls are bluish in tone, so were the walls of Mrs. Maimba's bedroom. The initial therapy therefore lay with bringing Mrs. Maimba to surroundings that kept all the memory of her bedroom out of her mind. Her husband was the other factor that required banishment from her side as this exacerbated the problem. Dr Ndetei changed the lighting to orange and then continued with his psycho-analysis.

Mrs. Maimba stayed in the Maya Carberry for two weeks during which no nurses or Mr. Maimba were allowed near her. Dr Ndetei held two hourly discussions with her during which he managed to convince her that human beings were similar to other mammals in their sexual habits, except perhaps the privacy which shrouds human relationships.

On seeing Mr. Maimba, however, he prescribed that their home required being manned by male servants so as to keep memories of that fateful day far away from his wife. Their bedroom was also to receive a face-lift with a different bed, sheets and wall colour, very different from the original blue. It was only after these changes were effected that it was found safe to release Mrs. Maimba.

I had observed Nderu grow in 10 years into a modern town. In 1974 it had a double of every market facility. Shops, bars, butcheries, provision stores, tailoring shops, shoe-makers, vegetable stalls, *busaa* clubs, tea kiosks, a Catholic church and a Protestant one. There were two charcoal stalls, two regular buses and even two watch dogs. In 10 years, all these had increased tenfold and she now had the Salvation Army, Independent Church, *Akorino, Wa Mathina*, Orthodox, P.C.E.A., Legio Maria and the Church of the Province of Kenya all having shelters for worship at Nderu. The *busaa* clubs were no more, but instead 10 beer drinking shops were all over Nderu, several tailors' shops, two food "take-aways", a steel rolling factory making all sorts of ironware, several buses plied Nairobi-Nderu and the town had a police station. The East African Community research station now renamed Kenya Agricultural Research Institute had many Kenyans donning white lab-coats roaming around Nderu. Besides a large male population of job-seekers from all over the Republic, single women joined the Nderu community as barmaids, market-stall attendants or as ordinary flirts. The former *busaa* clubs had been turned into lodging rooms and the two bars had become boarding and lodging houses. The northern side overlooking the Ondiri river developed into a *Majengo*, the name Kenyans gave to estates made of make-shift houses constructed with mud, cartons and brambles that characterized all old and new Kenyan towns.

Nderu Police Station was kept fairly busy by Nderu *Majengo*, which housed men and women of all manner of trades. There were pimps, gigolos, bang and illegal brew peddlers and Nairobi brothel inmates who would escape from Nairobi when the going became tough and returned to it during the first weeks of months. This migratory behaviour was conducted with a precision of the famous migratory birds and was well known to the police, the general public of Nderu and even our clinic.

I had known Dr Gichua Gikere whom Nderu people simply referred to as "Dr GG", for a year now. Nderu had tolled a monthly metamorphic cycle within him. He was all energy from every 28th of the month, whistled loudly as he went about his business and wore impeccably clean clothes particularly, with a legendary bow-tie. This continued until the tenth day of every month. Between the eleventh and nineteenth, he drunk much more, was less serious and tended to turn into a joker full of clowning behaviour. The period twentieth to twenty-seven, Dr GG abandoned the ship, opening Nderu Clinic for only four hours, playing truant and leaving the place very much unattended to. He also drunk heavily during this period, largely through a credit facility he had maintained for a decade at the Mama Njeri's bar. He had during one of those 20th to 27th periods been found by drug inspectors in a stupor and when awakened, begun fumbling with syringes. He was about to inject one of the baffled inspectors when the stare of Steve Maranga brought him back to earth.

"I am not sick doctor! I am the drugs inspector from KCH!" Maranga shouted. Dr GG froze.

* * *

The police station had been upgraded into a full station in 1973 during the 10th anniversary of Kenyan Independence. It had remained an out-post of Kikuyu for over two decades having been opened as a Mau Mau screening camp since 1953. Within a year of its promotion it had obtained most of the facilities of a police station. It consisted of one building with six rooms — the report office, inspector Kamundia's office, the crime office, traffic office, the cell and the water-closet. Behind it was a courtyard where mangled accident vehicles were lumped in two groups, those which had caused fatal and non-fatal catastrophes. In front of the main building was a public car park and the Black Maria, the van that was used exclusively for mass arrests and transportation of suspects, was parked. The rest of the two-acre piece of land composed of dome-like structures made of galvanised iron sheets, which housed the policemen and two, two-bedroom modern houses in which the inspectors lived. Inspector Paul Wekesa was in-charge of the crime branch at Nderu. He stood six feet and an inch. He was now thirty eight, fifteen of which he had put into in the Kenya Police. After attending High School from which he passed his school certificate with a third division, he joined the police after going through a six months' course in Kiganjo, Nyeri. He had learnt what" Service to All" (the Kenya Police motto), meant and was extremely devoted to his work.

I first met Paul Wekesa in a bar at Kikuyu a year after I had begun visiting Nderu. Dr GG had taken me to Kikuyu to have a drink when this tall, dark, clean shaven officer walked in and saluted *daktari*, the swahili version he preferred for Dr GG. He had bright eyes, smiled sparingly but had a firmness about him that was obvious to anyone who looked at him.

"*Bwana* Inspector, please join us," Dr GG called.

"Sorry *daktari*, I am a bit of in a hurry. Have you seen Chief Inspector Kamundia?"

"Not in a few weeks. Please meet Dr Munguti my colleague at Nderu?"

"Oh," Inspector Wekesa said shaking my hand,"You mean they wean doctors now at an early age?"

"Why, what do you mean?"

"I have not yet met a twenty year-old *daktari*."

I certainly did not look twenty, but Inspector Wekesa must have been used to older men as doctors. Occasionally I had been told that I looked much older than my actual twenty-nine years.

"You can have one *bwana* Inspector." Dr GG insisted then called the waiter, ordered two Exports for Inspector Wekesa. Apparently the inspector had such great respect for Dr GG that he could not resist the Exports but he emphasised that he had to leave as soon as he had the two.

After he had left us, Dr GG told me a little bit about the Inspector.

"Wekesa is a good man although a cop. His heart is as clean as a syringe. However, as in all public jobs one cannot please everyone. To Wekesa, police work is a religion. He cannot visualize a world without cops," Dr GG finished.

At times they would have spirited arguments on the supremacy of those jobs that entailed law and order. Wekesa equated the police to the tenets of the country as friction is to the universe. If anyone doubted the value of the force, one was advised to consider a frictionless world — a world with no brakes, bodies colliding repeatedly against each other in the universe, Inspector Wekesa would argue. It was to him, a chaotic situation such as all hell breaking loose.

Wekesa was extremely conscientious. For the fourteen years he had been in the police force he had never taken to bribe, those who knew him, claimed. He worked hard, pursuing crime trails relentlessly until he had found either the dead abyss of it, or unravelled and brought whoever was responsible to book.

1973 was a type of turning point in the country. A few cops had started taking bribes to let off crimes, cause report files to go missing or advise criminals on how to conceal whatever they were arrested of. Paul Wekesa was the maverick of Nderu, adamant, duty conscious and the man of the law. To him there was no nobler job than that of ensuring that the land had LAW and ORDER and no-one compromised the provisions of the Penal Code in particular.

"Can you imagine a world governed by rapists, pimps, prostitutes, thieves, murderers all running loose?" he would confront dissenting voices.

"But surely this can be said even of sewers," Dr GG would insist without wanting to bring about the argument on the equal importance of some, such as himself who treated gonorrhoea and other ailments.

"I will only speak for the job I know," Wekesa would say. "I do not know about the sewerage department, but they do not appear to impact on Nderu or even Kikuyu. As for the Police

Station — well I am sure you know what I am talking about Dr GG."

Dr Gichua Gikere had been a clinical assistant for the past thirty years. In the second world war he had ministered to men in Korea and Burma where the British engaged the Italian forces. On returning from Burma he joined the Kenyan Government service in the then King George Hospital from which he believed he acquired all there was to learn about medicine. He was convinced he could handle any medical problem — Asthma, recurrent gonorrhoea, sinusitis, arthritis and all those things he referred to as the King George puzzles.

"Never tell a patient you are referring him to another place," he would admonish you. "The days when Kikuyu medicine-men asked the sick person's escort to fold the goat-hide because the subject belonged to them and God, are gone. Even Governor Wallace had to go to a Chinese acupuncturist to get off of his wheel-chair. If he came to Nderu, the cure-all clinic, he would walk the following day," Dr GG boasted.

Dr GG, at sixty-nine, was extremely courageous and stoic. He circumcised boys, removed Luos' six teeth that required this form of initiation, tattooed, ear pierced and even ear-lobe carved those Masai's that required this form of ritual. However, his speciality and one he performed with a lot of joy was to help mothers who needed help without the blessing of the government and to the chagrin of the Pope — whom he disdainfully referred to as the "God's hypocrite."

He had seen a nine-year old, beget a baby in Burma and had vowed never to let any human being suffer a child one does not want. After - all, before the white man came to Kenya, he reasoned, young women belonging of all Kenyan shades, secretly had foeticide performed in all manner of ways to save them embarrassment.

I am not sure I could describe Dr Gichinga as a mean man. He paid my salaries every month although I always had to demand it. Dr GG never asked to be paid, he paid himself out of our monthly takings. Whether it was the actual sum or not I did not know but his boozing appeared disproportionate with the two thousand shillings he claimed, Dr Gichinga owed him monthly. When I got broke, I would be tempted to pay myself just as Dr GG but I so much feared being caught by my employer. I wanted to be a nice, honest doctor who lived within his means. Our charges began at thirty shillings for most ailments requiring injections. These were mainly the less serious sexually transmitted, septic wounds and some coughs and colds that were proving difficult to ordinary counter mixtures. More complicated ailments were referred to the P.C.E.A. Hospital near the Church of Torch at Kikuyu.

Nduku could not understand how I could be broke.

"Dr Omoro is now driving a new VW," she begun. "And he graduated the other day from an Indian Medical School," she added.

"Nyamboga has moved to Parklands," she continued. "And he is a mere Assistant in Hamilton, Harrison and Matthews."

I do not know why Mary Nduku's taunts had so much effect on me. I hated being weighed against my peers but perhaps Nduku knew how effective such taunts could be. She would look at my defiant face, recoil and groan that if I never aspired for wealth, I should have remained in Tala and not so much struggled for a medical degree.

She was in a way right. Everyone was trying to make money in Kenya during those days. It mattered little how one made it, but money seemed to be the thing for everyone.

Dr Gichinga came that morning complaining of a two hundred shillings' fee for a dental treatment.

"Can you imagine Omoro torturing me for forty-five minutes with those damned metallic gadgets, then slapping a two-hundred shillings' bill on me?" he fumed. "These dentists are crazy!"

Dr Omoro was one of the few Kenyans who had ventured into dentistry. Unfortunately or fortunately for dentists, not many Kenyans visited their private surgeries except perhaps those from the higher income groups. The dentists therefore had only a few clients, but whenever any entered their dens, they made sure they compensated for less patients by charging high.

"Can you imagine that guy has his own X-ray machine?" Dr Gichinga continued. "And he can afford the five thousand shillings' rent at the Mansion House," he added.

I believe it was then that Dr Gichinga considered to open a second clinic in Nairobi. He, however, chose River Road instead of the more posh area of central Nairobi.

* * *

Our clinic was soon to be a hub of activity. It stood in the middle of Campos Ribeiro Road. Next to us was the Wakarinu Lodge, the Nairobi House of pleasure. Within walking distance, were other day and night-clubs such as Wendandu, Nyanza, Amani, Halian's and Masharubu's.... Among these were guest houses that specialised in charging for siestas by men and women and seemed most popular places with the burgeoning Nairobi male population. Some four buildings from River Road Clinic, was the Wananchi Pharmacy and adjacent to it was Dr and Dr (Mrs.) Patel's Clinic which specialised in gynaecological problems.

I soon came to learn from Dr Gichinga how Nderu and River Road Clinics would complement each other. In Nairobi where the law was most vigilant, some operations could not be quietly, albeit illegally, performed. These included abortions, baby sales and storage of contraband drugs and equipment. On the other hand, business especially for the sexually transmitted diseases boomed in Nairobi River Road where many patients who contacted either syphilis or gonorrhoea would rather pay as much as a hundred shillings for Penicillin injections instead of visiting KCH or even the notorious sexually transmitted diseases' clinic, opposite the famous River Road Casino. In Nderu while the takings were low because of a generally low income rural population, the clinic would act as the referral clinic for those maladies that required being done far from the long arm of the law. I was supposed to attend to the River Road Clinic, but occasionally visit the Nderu one for those more complicated medical cases.

Dr GG continued as the doctor in-charge at Nderu but only visited Nairobi to either purchase medicines or consult with Dr Gichinga. He was never to administer at the River Road Clinic.

It was a usual chilly July morning when three men brought three compact wooden crates into the River Road Clinic.

"Dr Waweru Gichinga asked that we deliver these here," said one of the porters as he placed the crates at the patient's waiting room. They appeared fairly heavy but I did not bother to ask what the contents were. Later in the day, Dr Gichinga telephoned and asked me if the goods had been delivered. It was at that time he said he had finally managed to buy an X-ray machine. I was terribly overjoyed because I now knew that our work was to be far easier, besides being more lucrative. Dr Gichinga however, cautioned that we were not as yet to broadcast the new acquisition as he did not want the bank that had lent him money to know where this machine was located. Although the explanation appeared highly suspect, I did not at the time bother about it, all I knew was that we were to treat the X-ray machine as a tool for our clinics only.

My first X-ray candidate was Jane Achieng a bulky thirty five years old Luo woman who came to the clinic with a broken nose.

"This man is an animal," she sobbed. "Can you imagine I was battered because I declined to act bestial?" she enquired.

I calmed her down, took an X-ray of her jaws and nose, then treated her left eye which seemed to have conjunctivitis from the blows, that must have been quite heavy. She then went on to narrate the sad story involving her and ex-army Major.

She had been told how nice Major Kombo was and that he gave cleaning jobs mainly to women irrespective of their tribes. All one needed to do was to visit his office at County Hall, attend to an interview and the job was hers. He was known not to take bribes like other Nairobi employers nor did he ask for many favours. All he would want, was to test that the job-seeker was energetic enough to slash grass, walk at least three kilometres everyday and was a deserving mother. Major Kombo was a really nice man. Real nice.

She had gone that Sunday morning to Ma or Kombo's office situated on the first floor. Her companion Gladys who showed her the way, had left and gone to work near the Ambassadeur Hotel. The man, aged about sixty years peeped through the door at the adjacent room where she sat awaiting him.

He beckoned her to enter the large executive hall that was well appointed. A city superintendent's office had to be anyway. He sat at the centre of the semi-circular executive table then asked for her particulars which included age, tribe, current occupation, marital status, number of children, period in the city and the part of the city she lived in. To all these she gave candid answers. That she was thirty-five, a Luo, unemployed, a third wife with two children and was resident at Ziwani for the past five years.

"What have you been doing in five years?" Major Kombo peremptorily asked, stunning Janet Achieng.

"Well, I sell *ngege* sometimes ....."

"What else? Start walking around the room!" the Major ordered. She started walking, mumbling that she also sold *sukuma wiki*, but was by and large a house-wife.

"Stop!" Major Kombo thundered. "Undress now!" He roared, stunning Achieng even further. For Achieng generally, stripping was not a major issue, since bathing in the lake and fishing during her childhood days involved undressing in public. However, Janet Achieng was not prepared for this in the Major's office. Gladys had not prepared her for this. She had, however, known that she may be subject to the possibility of offering certain bodily favours to the eccentric nice old man. She considered resisting the instruction but another voice urged her to see the interview through to the end. She therefore unbuckled her belt, started opening the front of her frock hoping the old man would request her to stop in the middle of the exercise. He did not, but continued to ogle at her. Out came the left hand which she used for holding the top left hand of her dress. Then came out her right side which she held similarly with the right hand. She then looked at the Major, full in the face to see if he would yield. Major Kombo's eye-lids dilated slightly more and she noticed that his mouth opened slightly. He did not speak. Twisting her lips a little bit, she let her dress fall, stepped out of it and stood facing the maniac, for further instructions. He raised his hands and pointed at her brassiere. This she also removed. Major Kombo continued to stare expecting more undressing. Janet Achieng now had only her half petticoat and a pair of knickers under her. She decided to go only as far as the petticoat and no further.

"You are to remove everything mama," Major Kombo softly but sternly warned making Janet wonder if she could survive this crazy interview.

She decided to proceed quickly with the affair, get over with her interview and then get out as quickly as she could. On removing her knickers, Major Kombo got even crazier asking her to start matching around the room while explaining that the job she was applying for, required stamina. She circled the room naked twice, then noticed what the old man really wanted.

She declined after which the old maniac set upon her face, ending with breaking her nose. Janet learnt afterwards that many other interviewees had gone through a similar ordeal because the old sadist got his erections through marching of naked women in front of him. I treated Janet Achieng and was tempted to call the police over Major Kombo, but realised that my part lay in administering to the sick and not in pressing for criminal prosecution over attempted rapes.

Inspector Wekesa called a meeting for all the twenty policemen of Nderu Police Station.

"I want all of you to think of anything strange that happened in the last one week concerning pregnant women, prostitutes, lovers, clinics and bars," he said flaming his eyes on the team that managed law and order in Nderu.

"What are we looking for *afendi*?" corporal Kiplangat asked.

"At this stage you are looking for anything unusual that may have occurred, I want written reports to me by eleven. You are dismissed." Inspector Wekesa ended the meeting.

This was the way my friend Joel Kiplangat described that morning's events when he called at my clinic. I had expected him to request for Tetracycline, the capsules that he often requested me to provide, but instead he came with events from Nderu.

"Dr Munguti, you were in Nderu on Wednesday night. Who is the lady you were entertaining at Mama Njeri's?"

"Oh, a client who wanted to see Dr Munguti?" I innocently said.

"She appeared pregnant."

"Oh yes, even pregnant women these days visit pubs. Why, has she done anything wrong?"

"No, but I would have wanted to ask her something."

"Well, she is from Tanzania but I don't know where she lives in Nairobi. She has visited here one or two times, otherwise the one who knows her better is my employer."

"Dr Waweru Gichinga?"

"Yes, at Ward Twenty, of KCH."

"Thank you Dr Munguti, let us have a drink together sometime," Kiplangat said, then left.

I had visited Nderu on Wednesday, with Halima, the Bukoba broad, who sought Dr GG's assistance over her family planning nightmare. At 9.00 a.m. I had left her with Dr GG, then driven in Crispus' (the local forester's) car to Kikuyu. On Thursday, Dr GG had rang me and asked me to visit Nderu for a celebration. I indulged the old man by closing the River Road Clinic at 3.00 p.m. and boarding the Nakuru-bound bus that took me to the Zambezi from which I walked to Nderu. We spent the evening at the clinic drinking, ripped goat meat and sung all those folklore songs that accompanied Kikuyu feasts in the olden days. Dr GG made me understand that he had performed his miracle perfectly and saved a Bukoba prostitute from committing suicide by terminating her problems and a pregnancy. I did not ask how it was done, but I knew, it must have involved complicated surgery for which I doubted Nderu Clinic's or its doctor's capability. I did, however, observe that Dr GG was unusually jittery, clumsy and not quite himself. He had slaughtered the goat inside the clinic, left the hoofs, head and the white skin in the medicine store, carelessly left blood marks all over the four walls of the clinic and not even bothered cleaning the examination couch that he had used for butchering the goat. Everything appeared quite bizarre but I associated this with the old man's advancing senility.

Wekesa himself came to my clinic on Friday morning. He wanted to know all I knew about the "feast" we had at the clinic on Thursday. I told him all I knew but also demanded to know what all this questioning was all about. Had we done wrong by slaughtering a goat in the clinic or was it the singing till one o'clock in the morning? He promised to let me know all there was in the next few days.

On Sunday morning, Nduku with whom I had shared the night woke me up.

"There are men from the C.I.D., who want you. What have you done?"

"I've done nothing." All the doctors attached to KCH had gone on strike and I had read that week of, doctors being arrested all over the Republic. I was therefore expecting my detention as a matter of course. I dressed casually and told Nduku to keep the arresting officers company.

"We have a few things we would like you to assist us in, at the Police Station, Dr Munguti."

"Which things?"

"Well, a few medical puzzles," the taller sterner looking cop said.

It was at Kileleshwa Police Station where I learnt that a homicide inquiry was taking place because a foetus had been collected at the District Forest Officer's compound at Nderu; a hand of a female adult on the road leading to the Forest Station; and ten other pieces of a headless female body had been collected at equidistant intervals all the way to the forest labourers' village called Nguriunditu. The female body pieces and the clothes recovered, Corporal Kiplangat of Nderu had reported, appeared to belong to a lady Dr Munguti had been seen drinking with at Mama Njeri's bar in Nderu, on Wednesday night. I was therefore to make a statement on this lady although she had not been reported as missing. Just a statement, so I thought. But in the end, this would turn out to be the most harrowing and bone chilling experience I have ever had in my life.

Dr Gichinga had denied any knowledge of Halima so had Dr GG, thus putting me in an extremely embarrassing situation. Dr GG said that he received many female clients for different maladies he could never disclose. All the information Dr Gichinga and Gichua Gikere acquired about their patients was confidential.

I told all I knew about Halima save the issue of seeking for an abortionist. I told the police of how she had told me of coming from Bukoba, mother of five starving kids, currently selling her body at Pumwani - *Majengo*. She had come to Nderu to visit a friend and when she got sick at Mama Njeri's I referred her to Nderu Clinic at nine o'clock.

Wekesa was smarter. He visited Nderu Clinic and ordered a forensic search which revealed that the body parts and the foetus had actually been in Nderu Clinic. The problem, however, arose because there was no report on a missing person, no records with the Immigration Department of a Tanzanian living in *Majengo* and missing. In utter desperation he came to me and asked me what I thought he should do. Chief Inspector Kamundia, he had a gut feeling, had been bribed by Dr GG and Dr Gichinga, because he had that morning harangued him for having made a search of Nderu Clinic. The place was a haven for those sick with VD, Kamundia had said and Wekesa had wasted fifty policeman-days looking for a phantom. Four more foetuses and three skulls had been discovered in the bush and dust-bins!

I calmed poor Wekesa and asked him to store the knowledge he had, until an inquiry or murder trial required it. Although I could not tell Kamundia or anyone else, I too felt there was something wrong with Dr GG and my employer's denial of the knowledge of Halima. As the days went by and Halima ceased to feature in either our discussions or in River Road Clinic, I got convinced Paul Wekesa may not have been chasing a rainbow. One day I woke up sweating profusely from a wild dream that Dr GG was serving us Halima's roasted-ribs.

My internship had been concluded over a year before. I had worked in Nderu Clinic for some 13 months and now was fully in-charge of the River Road one. I no longer worked in KCH even if I continued to draw a salary which Dr Gichinga ensured I got, to avoid having to pay me higher. Life was good. I had now a driving license and could afford an old car, to enable me travel to Tala.

I had not in all those two and a half years returned to Tala. I had religiously observed my promise of never entering a *Matatu* for my birth place. I was, when I revisited it, going to make a triumphal entry in my own car!

My mother, father, brothers and sisters, however, continued to see me in Nairobi wherever there was need. It was mostly when money was short, crops had failed and school fees were required. My mother was the least demanding because she never asked for anything from me. The only thing she wanted was that I grow into a nice man who never mixed with wicked Nairobi women, but lived to marry a nice Kamba girl who would bear for me ten kids. This she always told me whenever she met me.

She had come to Nairobi the previous December, suffering from some rheumatic pains. I had referred her to Dr Gichinga as I did not wish to examine my own mother but he referred her to GG whom I could not trust. I therefore took up the matter but could not proceed when I had to ask her to open her bosom for the heart-beat examination. "You are a doctor and not her son now," I had told myself and nearly asked her to remove her dress and lie on the examination bed.

Dr Patel came to my rescue although it cost me quite a bit in spite of the fact that I used River Road Clinic funds for it. At that time I rationalised that since I was entitled to free medical attention by Dr Gichinga and he had accepted to look after my mother, there was no harm in using his funds for the same purpose. After all he had referred her to his own clinic in Nderu. When I looked at it further, I had to accept that it was my first act of larceny I had committed against my employer and it disturbed me. "Two hundred and fifty shillings, paid to Dr Patel the gynaecologist four blocks from us, for a job I could have done....Anyway that is life...." I told myself and buried it in the store of my memory.

* * *

At the beginning of the third week of January, Dr GG came to River Road Clinic accompanied by a beautiful young lady of about twenty years.

"Meet My daughter Mumbi," Dr GG began when he noticed my stare of surprise. "Dr Munguti, the young doctor the whole family has been longing to see."

I was so enchanted by her bright eyes, spindle thin and very lovely chocolate skin body, not quite the colour of Mary Nduku but just about her tone. I had known that GG had six children all of whom I had not yet met. He often talked about them but for some reasons had kept them away from me. He had often talked about Mumbi who worked in Mombasa and I had come to realise that she was his favourite child. Two of the children a boy and a girl, were in school in Kitale while the oldest daughter and son lived in Voi where they had grown up and worked, Wambui was a nurse and Kiragu a truck driver. Only Kariuki lived in Nderu with the mother but he spent all his days at the Sigona Club as a caddy. I often met Mrs. GG, at the local pub where she would sometimes accompany the old man for a drink.

"How do you do Miss Gichua?" I said as I extended my hand at her. I could not help feeling the warmth with which she held my hand. She looked at me tartly as if to invite me to cast my doctor's official greetings aside and treat her like a woman.

60

"My dad has talked a lot about you," she said. "And you must come to Nderu now that I am there," she added. I could not mistake the sincerity and challenge the invitation suggested.

I gave Dr GG his share of the medicines that had come with Dr Gichinga, I showed him round the new X-ray machine room then promised to visit them the following weekend. Saturday afternoons were my days off, especially since Nairobi, other than at the end of the months, appeared to go to sleep during the weekends.

"I'll be expecting you," Dr GG's daughter shot as they left, giving me what I thought was a wink.

* * *

The Nakuru-bound OTC bus stopped at my usual stop, by the Petrol Station and I disembarked for my umpteenth time to make my two-kilometre walk to Nderu. I was by now so used to this stretch that I could literally make it blindfolded by counting all the stops from Race-course Road, Westlands, Uthiru, Kinoo, Muthiga then Zambezi Motel.

The Nairobi-Nakuru bound passengers were of different shapes, sizes and carried all sorts of parcels and loads. As I looked at all these people, I had all sorts of feelings. The women travelled daily to Nairobi to vend vegetables only to return in the evenings with sugar, cooking fat and other manufactured items required for their households. The men travelled everyday from Nderu to Nairobi to work in the construction sites and earn a salary that they left behind in the bars, *busaa* clubs, the brothels or whore-houses of *Majengo*. Others who had wives and kids to look after would struggle to return home with some savings to ensure that the families were fed, clothed and may be, educated. All these flashed in my mind as I trekked from Zambezi to Nderu, where I arrived at 2.00 o'clock.

Mumbi, Dr GG's daughter, was waiting for me all right. Her old man had gone home but had asked that I man the clinic on his behalf. However, since it was past two o'clock, I could close and go for *nyama choma* at Mama Njeri's bar or have drinks brought to the clinic while the meat roasted. She appeared to have arranged everything about how I would spend the afternoon. I noticed that she had been drinking.

"I will be leaving at five, though," I said non-commitally leaving her to decide whether to close the clinic or not.

"No, you will not. This clinic can make an excellent boarding house," she teased rubbing her father's examination bed in a suggestive manner I did not quite approve. Mumbi was quite headstrong as I came to learn later. She had no doubts on what she intended to do with me and this made me feel uncomfortable.

"How come you are not yet married?" she started, making me even more unnerved.

"Please go and bring me a White Cap and whatever you want for yourself," I told her trying to avoid a subject a lot of people wanted me to discuss. I gave her some fifty shillings and after she left, I also begun wondering why at thirty I was not even contemplating marriage. Irene at KCH had also asked me a similar question, but I had rebuffed her by asking why she too had not yet married.

People married for three things, I had heard a preacher before solemnizing a marriage say; for companionship, for children and for fun. I was already getting fun with Mary Nduku. Children as yet, I did not require and my companionship came from the many patients who brought all sorts of problems to me at the River Road Clinic.

Mumbi returned with three White Caps and two Pilsners, which she adeptly opened and placed on Dr GG's consultation table. She sat on her father's examination bed and I on the chair which I felt as if we were desecrating with beer. She looked at me as she sipped her Pilsner, began dangling her right leg then as if she was not to give up she resumed her cross-examination.

"Why, I asked you, you are not married?"

"I cannot marry."

"Why?"

"I do not know what to do with a wife yet."

"What do people do with wives?"

"They make them pregnant, get babies and watch these grow."
I said.

"And you cannot do that."

"No."

"I could show you how to do it," she challenged.

"When I am ready," I retorted.

"My father tells me you are a Mkamba and Kambas are famous
for these things."

"I am a Kamba but may be not as good as the others," I said.

I was shy with women, always waited until I was absolutely
sure I would succeed with a relationship and often scared by the
forthright, Mumbi's type that probed, challenged and egged me on.

We continued drinking. I cleared my three White Caps, she
her Pilsner, ate some roasted beef that Mumbi had ordered, then
closed the clinic. We proceeded to Mama Njeri's bar where we
found a lot of people unlike other twentieth of the month days. I
noticed four men that I had once treated of VD and three women
who had visited the clinic when I was manning Nderu Clinic.

"Where have you been doctor?" James Mwaura shouted from
one of the corners.

"Ah! Dr Munguti, you have come to see us!" a voice I could
not tell whose, bellowed.

"*Daktari*, welcome to Nderu," Dr GG shouted standing from
where he sat drunkenly and beckoning to his daughter and I.
"Mama Njeri, Mama Njeri, a crate of beer for Dr Munguti!" He
commanded.

The 12½ litres' crate of White Cap was placed before me by the
dutiful Mama Njeri's waitress. Then the boozing commenced, with
her acting as my maid. Dr GG had insisted that I was to clear the
whole crate before anyone else touched it, meaning that I was to
share with no-one. I obediently accepted this but knew only too
well that I could not absorb 12 litres of White Cap even if I stayed
in the bar until the following morning.

I asked for a Pilsner for Mumbi, then ordered five Tuskers for
Dr GG telling the waiter to give the old man "*guoko*" (the Kikuyu's
name for the token given) in return for an over-generous purchase
of booze for one.

"You realized I have beautiful daughters for whom I should be awarded?" he teased apparently unaware that he was making fairly serious prophecies as the events following our visit to Mama Njeri with his daughter, came to prove.

James Mwaura I came to discover was a clown. He made all sorts of jokes that some considered naughty though they gleed with mirth. He appeared particularly keen on matrimonial incompatibility and moot litigation over divorces. One man, Mwaura said, presented a petition to the court over his marriage.

"I had not expected a bucket from my wife your honour," he (the litigant) bellowed.

"Yes," the defiant defendant retorted. "Your honour the facts of an existing bucket may be true but you will appreciate that these things are relative. What do you expect of a lizard's tail inside the pants of the man who took one to the altar?"

A decree *nisi* was granted the petitioner, Mwaura concluded, making everyone writhe with guffaws of laughter as we watched him mimic the plaintiff's gesture raising the right little finger and waving it in the magistrate's eyes.

"Yes your honour, if this little gadget was all you were to give to your woman, what do you expect?"

John Okoth could not be outwitted by Mwaura. He joined with another regarding some two men of the Sikh community who had visited the Florida one day to collect some Kikuyu girls for a night's company. Wanjiku had appeared really drunk but Jessi urged his companion to make her dead drunk before they took her to bed. This was the only way to ensure she accepted the two men's terms. It was agreed that they would both enjoy her at the double price of two hundred shillings.

"What about VD?" the younger man who had not bought the services of a prostitute before protested.

"Simply open her legs and place a few drops of lemon in the vulva just before entering her," Jessi advised his companion. They drove to the Parklands flat which they shared with another member of the family, stretched Wanjiku on the bed then proceeded to cut the slices of lemon. Jessi helped his companion peel off Wanjiku's knickers, which easily came out, however, when his companion came to drip in the lemon juice, he nearly fainted when the lady who had appeared lifeless, asked him if he thought a female part was a *sambusa* (the triangular minced meat pie commonly eaten by Asians).

We boozed, laughed, talked until the late hours of the night. I looked at my watch and saw it was twelve midnight. Dr GG had somehow disappeared by this hour but their daughter who was dead drunk had her heavy head on my laps while Mama Njeri's bloodshot eyes and constant yawning told us all, it was time to wind up.

"Unless you people want Wekesa's Black Maria for a ride tonight, you better finish." Mama Njeri gave us the cue.

"Let us go." Mumbi commanded, yawning loudly and out-stretched her beautiful hands. I told Mama Njeri to "stock" my unfinished programme of nine bottles of beer, took Mumbi's hand and walked her to Nderu Clinic. There were no discussions over what we were to do.

At the clinic, I noticed, a place for sleeping had been arranged. On the floor was a mattress, clean sheets, blankets and a pillow, all ready for our heavy heads. Dr GG's consultation furniture — table, chair and even the examination couch were all squeezed at a corner. I was about to ask who had arranged all this, when something told me, I required to be more diplomatic than ask. I stripped all my clothes out, a sleeping practice I had acquired in the hot and humid equatorial climate of Ibadan but quite inappropriate in the cold of Nderu, then noticed Dr GG's daughter do likewise. She removed her black skirt, red blouse, kicked off her white shoes but left on her intimate apparel.

"For the doctors' hands, you fool!" she mockingly told me then joined me in the hard floor bed.

In all the days I administered medicine to Nderu people, I did not indulge in sex with any member of the community. I could watch beautiful barmaids come to the clinic, nervously explain that they were having pains in the back or that they did not know why they were having painful menstruation experiences. On examination I would often diagnose gonorrhoea and proceed with penicillin injections mainly in their bottoms. As a doctor I would honor my doctor-client relationship and act professionally even when seductively invited by some.

I am not sure of all what happened to me that night. All I remember is that in our drunken stupor, Mumbi gave me the greatest challenge that Mombasa must have taught her about romance. She made my days at Ibadan appear really second-rate coquetry. They were five years with only a year of a steady love-relationship with Gladys (a Ugandan nurse who had attended a year's course in nutrition with us). The rest of my time there, I was on the two-naira' diet encounters in the Mokola brothels. It is no wonder then, that I missed such simple things as bums rubbing and many others that required lack of scruples. In all, I would doubtless account that Mumbi was well versed in the act.

"You are not my doctor man, take me!" she screamed at me, pulling and hurting my hair.

My first medical ethics problem confronted me on a Monday afternoon. I was happy with River Road. I already had six thousand shillings in my Barclays Bank savings account. I could easily afford a deposit for a car, with the rest of the money, loaned by the government which granted these to the Senior Civil Servants. My patients were happy with my work, for they streamed into the clinic. At times as many as twenty men and women sat at the reception desk each willing to come and consult me. I had grown used to the routine questions and answers.

"I am passing painful urine," the men would start.

"Can I see," I would ask those who appeared less shy.

"When were you last with a woman?"

"Three days ago."

"OK, get on the couch and remove your trousers."

With the women the interview was slightly different.

"Doctor I have a painful back."

"Any discharge?"

"No."

"Do you notice anything unusual on your knickers?"

"Yes."

"Any pain when urinating?"

"Yes."

"Can I have some urine for examination?"

I would ask the stubborn ones to come the following day after examination results even when I was certain they had been infected with VD.

This particular Monday, I was relaxing reading of a Canberra doctor who was specialising in sex problems. Dr Mary Stewart had been interviewed by the *Time* magazine on why she had thought sexology had a place in modern medicine.

She asserted that the Australian men are terribly chauvinistic. The pioneer history whereby they travelled to strange lands as convicts, were left to fend for themselves, forcibly taking native Aborigine women, must be the source of this. Today all homes have problems because the women want love not pushing around for sexual encounters. What do the Australian men do? They go to Thailand for brides. And the women take on the Zimbabweans, South Africans, Italians, Greeks and other minorities that make them feel women, Mary Steward felt. For this reason Australia has a terrible social problem that can only be righted by sexologists who produce in lovers their Romeo and Juliet qualities, otherwise suppressed.

Earlier while at Ibadan I had read that Americans had actually set up special hospitals where men and women with sexual problems visited for education in the sexual act. Unfortunately most of these ended up getting abused and becoming camouflaged brothels. I could not however, find any faults with sex hospitals that became sex shops. Was there, I wondered, any difference between buying sex and buying sexual therapy? I was in the middle of these thoughts when a plump, richly dressed lady who appeared familiar, opened the door.

"My name is Eunice," she said in perfect English. "I hope you can help me," she added.

"I will do all I can madam," I said, slightly taken aback by this richly dressed lady who I made to be around forty years old. She certainly was not of the River Road category as evidenced by her sweet smelling and expensive perfume, extremely well manicured finger-nails and stiletto shoes that denoted good living.

"I am feeling terribly fatigued and my whole body is taut. My gynaecologist has failed to identify any problem."

"Any specific areas?"

"Yes, my back, my legs and even the neck?"

"How long has this been?"

"Most of this year, but I did not think it was a medical problem."

"Whom have you seen?"

"In the past Mr. Zimmermann has handled all my medical problems."

Robert Zimmermann was the leader in medicine in Nairobi. He was the best paid of the private gynaecologists having a clinic on the sixth floor of the prestigious Bruce House. Here was Eunice hoping a one year old doctor, Joseph Munguti, would help her. My *"Titanic"* had definitely appeared.

I was in the middle of these thoughts when the telephone rang.

"Waweru Gichinga here, is that you Dr Munguti?"

"Yes, Dr Gichinga," I reciprocated.

"Has Mrs. Maimba come to see you?"

"Mrs. who?" Then I saw my patient nodding in the affirmative. "Yes she is here."

"Take good care of her." He suddenly hang up without further information.

I examined my patient as thoroughly as I could to find out what her strange malady could be. Her heart-beat was normal for a forty-five years old lady, so was her blood-pressure. She had neither temperature nor any visible signs of the gynaecological problems affecting middle aged women.

"Mrs. Maimba, when was your last MP?"

"One year ago."

"How is your stool?"

"I have not had diarrhoea for years."

"And your urine?"

"Clear."

"Do you play any games."

"I recently began visiting the Hilton Health Club for some gymnastics and sauna."

"How recent was that."

"A week or so, ago."

I did not appear to get far with the cross-examination of Mrs. Maimba, so I decided to conduct some clinical tests. I asked her for some urine, stool and blood specimens then asked her to return after three days when I expected results of her examination to be available.

"You will see they are okay!" she said then gave me a coquettish giggle that seemed to dare me discover any serious condition in her.

"We shall see you in three days time Mrs. Maimba," I said, hoping she would leave and I continue with my patient, a male who was worried over the chancre he had. She however, did not go. Mrs. Maimba had knocked, entered without waiting for my assent, then placed on the table, her stool and urine specimens.

"My gynae examined these," she added fondling her breasts. "And I wish you would direct your eyes, young man to these areas instead of my stomach."

I was getting a bit touchy over the insinuation that I was not doing my job properly, although I must confess, I had not thought of a gynaecological issue with Mrs. Maimba. My clientele in the River Road Clinic, had been so far on extremely simple diseases, candidiasis, trichomoniasis, syphilis, malaria, etc. Rarely did healthy home-makers from the upper income brackets visit my clinic with healthy bodies that hid what was troubling them. I asked my chancre patient to dress and wait at the reception.

"Mrs. Maimba, why do you have this notion that, I am not doing as well as I should?"

"Waweru, assured me that you would be extremely thorough and take far more interest in my condition than they can at KCH"

"Who is Waweru?"

"Gichinga."

I could have fainted. The thought that my employer had referred her to me and she was now finding me wanting, perturbed me. I was however not to be outwitted by nagging women who had not been near a medical school.

"I would have wanted to examine you on Thursday, after the stool, urine and blood tests, but if you prefer today, you get on that couch and undress," I commanded her, wore my gloves, took my speculum and started on things I had left behind years ago at the University College of Ibadan, Medical School.

I examined every part of Mrs. Maimba, who had obeyed me and stripped off all her clothes leaving only her gold rings in the nose, fingers and ears. The bangles, neck and leg laces were also made of pure gold. Although I was not a jeweller I made that the lady was wearing not less than fifty thousand shillings' worth of golden and diamond ornaments. Her teeth, nose, mouth, eyes, armpits, pubis, hands, legs and all were in perfect condition. There were no lesions, warts or even rashes in her private parts and not a single pimple in any part of her body. I had in fact never seen such a healthy condition in a human being, male or female.

"Well, as far as I can tell, you are the most perfect living creature I have ever examined," I said, removing my gloves and asking Mrs. Maimba to dress up and give us the time we required for the clinicals.

"You seriously mean I am nice, doctor?"

"I give you a bill of clean health."

She shot me another disturbing romantic grin as she dressed, applied her make-up, reddening her lips rather prominently then left in a swagger.

* * *

Eunice Maimba came back on Thursday afternoon at exactly five o'clock. This was the time we normally closed the clinic and she appears to have timed her visit with this closure. All the other patients had dispersed and it was just as well because I did not want my patients to see a coquette who bullied me and did not care observing the code. She brought me some rose flowers and suggested that my wife ought to be laying some on my table every day.

"I am not yet privileged with a wife," I said, little knowing that I was signing my death warrant.

"Oh! you mean so handsome a man is not yet hooked?" she wondered dilating her eyes widely.

"Mrs. Maimba," I attempted to change the subject. "Your results are here and you are free of any organisms that cause human diseases. Just go, relax and enjoy your good health."

"You could help me relax?"

"Help you do what?" I asked.

"Relax and enjoy my good health?"

"One does not require help to enjoy oneself," I retorted believing it to be true.

"Oh, Dr Joseph Munguti, are you suggesting I am a hermaphrodite?" She entered into the world of academic discussions I loved and never succumbed to being outwitted in.

"No Mrs. Maimba, I am not asexual either, but I do not require help to enjoy myself."

"Is that so? How, do you masturbate?"

"I do not."

"How then can you say, you do not require anyone, to enjoy yourself?"

It then dawned upon me how naive I had been. I had believed that marriage gave everyone all the sexual satisfaction one required and that Eunice Maimba in her wonderful health was a contented mother with all that one would require in life.

This is how it all started. Mrs. Maimba and I had a relationship for the next one year, which nearly ruined both of us. We travelled all over the country on weekends, took long hours off work nesting at The Nice People's Rendezvous in Pangani. She was generous. Unlike Mary Nduku who depended on my meagre salary, she would pick most of our bills in expensive hotels. She even bought me suits! One evening she commanded me to wear a suit whose stripes I did not like. I was already a sugar boy with a sugar mummy!

Phil Ogunya was a vet, a graduate of Kabete campus and was now the District Veterinary Officer. I had met him one morning when he came to the River Road Clinic complaining of Dr GG. He knew me, he said, when I had attended to him at Nderu a year before, although I could not quite remember his bearded face. Dr GG had failed to control his ailment, in spite of having used a large veterinary syringe, with which he intra-muscularly injected 15 c.c. of penicillin which nearly killed Phil. I examined Phil's swollen buttocks out of the old man's injections, diagnosed a syphilitic chancre on his large phallus then advised him that I would try a new drug that had just entered the market which was to cure him. I administered procaine penicillin G in oil with aluminium monostreate and asked him to come for more after, every three-day interval. Four days later he came back with a poorly attired lady whom he introduced as his wife. He instructed me to treat her without mentioning what she may be suffering from.

Mrs. Phil protested, when the husband left. She said she had to be told what was wrong because all Phil had told her, was that they were sick and had to go to hospital. I did not know what to do, but merely asked for blood and urine specimens, then advised her to return after two days. Phil had promised to bring the consultation and treatment fees which amounted to some two hundred shillings, the following day, but he did not. His wife's results came on Thursday, but the blood tests showed no signs of treponemes. I had no benefit of either examining her genitalia or taking specimen from her labia, but would have as well proceeded with the assumption that Phil had infected her with the disease.

Without the clinic's dues, however, I could not provide Mrs. Phil with expensive medicines. This placed me in a most awkward situation. I told her the truth that I saw nothing wrong with her but the husband had to see me as soon as possible. Phil did not appear until after a week. He paid my fees but failed to put a deposit for his wife's treatment.

"I cannot treat your wife without her consent and I require to examine her genitalia to be able to tell how serious or otherwise her condition may be." I proffered.

"No, you cannot let her know."

"Then I may tell her that I am looking for sores."

"No you cannot do that."

"I am afraid you may not understand how serious the situation is. Untreated syphilis will not only kill your wife but re-infect you!" I warned him.

I could not understand how a person who had gone through university albeit veterinary could be so naive with regard to disease diagnosis and treatment. I had, however, to go through all these, because first I was bound by my profession to treat the sick without consideration, on the other hand, I had to protect my client's secrets and yet my employer's interests needed protection also. I was between the devil and the deep blue sea — of money and medical ethics.

"Okay, you pay two hundred shillings for her, I will see what to do about her," I asked Phil who protested vehemently that I had indicated the wife was not sick, though I now wanted money.

I treated Mr. and Mrs. Phil Ogunya for a few days after which I was certain that all the *Treponema pallidum* had been flushed out of their system. Two weeks later, Phil came to my clinic accompanied by an elderly lady whom I made to be about Mrs. Maimba's age.

"This is Naomi, please handle her the way you handled my wife." Then he left.

Naomi told me that she was a mother of five children, one who was a nurse at the KCH and that, Phil was a friend of her husband. She was having pains all over her genitals and had to tell a friend rather than the husband who could have whipped her if he knew of her sickness. I did not bother to find out from her what her relationship with Phil was as I knew it could not have been very different from that of mine and Mrs. Maimba. Naomi unlike Phil, had gonorrhoea which cured easily after three visits to the clinic.

Phil continued to see me and I believe a friendship developed between us. He would ring and ask if the human doctor wanted a drink with the dogs' doctor and I would oblige. He was an interesting man who told interesting stories. His life was full of peculiar episodes. He never liked a lovely woman, flower, compound, clothes or anything that glittered.

"All that glitters is not gold," he would admonish me now and then. "Look at clean money. It is as wicked as dirty money. It will buy a prostitute just as quickly." In a way he was an eccentric, who loved all the second-rate things. His shirt had to have a torn collar. The coat although clean, was always of the weather-beaten types. He did not believe in more money than was due to him and he put no more effort in anything than was necessary or justifiable.

"Take Naomi, for instance, she is married like me. Her husband does not satisfy her, as I do. I have to struggle if I need my wife. Why should I not prefer Naomi to Mrs. Phil?" He then let out a secret about the two women in his life. His particularly large body was liked by Naomi who harboured a secret that she was fathomless. The wife he had married had from the start not enjoyed his love-making and had lately denied him conjugation.

"Can you imagine that I had girls refer each other to me at Kabete," he bragged. "For instance there was this American woman who used to drag me out of classes, yet my own wife does not want me near her."

"Have you actually lately tried making love to her?" I enquired.

"Yes and my member cannot even penetrate her?"

"How about Naomi?"

"No problem."

The relationship between Phil and Naomi took a dramatic turn when Dr Gichinga called me to KCH, Ward Twenty, to help with a patient who was bleeding profusely from stab wounds. Irene was screaming hysterically and Dr Gichinga was cursing her to be firm with the thread. It was the strangest twist of fate I had so far seen. The man with the deep buttocks' wounds was my friend Phil Ogunya the lover of Naomi, Irene's mother and the wounds had been inflicted by Kamanja, Irene's father who had found them in his bed at South B.

"Can you imagine my mother coming here and swearing to me that Phil has shed blood for her and she'll never leave him?" Irene sobbed. "I hope you are not letting the police know."

"We are not on the beat here," Dr Gichinga said a fact he had emphasised many times before. "Our job is to administer to the sick even when they have wronged us."

Phil the "Hog" as I came to call him recovered from of his wounds although he took a whole month. Irene looked after him faithfully although she told me that when her father was beaten by her mother over the stabbing affair, she had felt like dosing Phil's lunch.

"You should put the cyanide in Gilbert's first," I taunted, a thing that I half-expected someone to one day, do.

I had decided to be a venereologist. So much was already happening to me to the River Road Clinic that I begun thirsting for more knowledge. The government had ordered doctors working in public hospitals to stop running private clinics. Dr Gichinga had asked me to resign my government job, but I declined. He himself was not relinquishing his government employment yet he ran two clinics. It was Dr Munguti, his employee that he preferred sacrificing.

I pored through books written on venereal diseases. I noticed that all of them had a moral slant towards the causes of VDs and all authors on the subject wrote about promiscuity and immorality as major causes of the spread. Monogamous stable relationships were advocated and recommended as preventive measures and prostitution vigorously condemned. The more I pondered over these issues, the more I got convinced that the moral stance contributed towards the failure to eradicate VDs and the costly nature with which their cure was associated. I thought that if we all opened up on sex matters and regarded gonorrhoea as an ordinary disease just like the common cold, for instance, infected persons would readily seek medical help. Public health centres and hospitals should make medicine more readily available and consequently each would cease being a hurdle to treatment. I felt that sufferers from VD were discriminated, ridiculed and made to feel embarrassed which resulted in their harbouring and spreading the disease consciously or unconsciously.

I visited the special treatment clinic on Cross Road hoping that since this centre was built to counter the social stigma on Venereal diseases, the attitude was different but I found the situation even worse. A patient was required to bring the sexual partner also along. If ever I ran the clinic, I swore, I would never require partners being brought. I would in addition strive to vindicate VDs as ordinary ailments discussed by patients. How to remove sex from the shackles of morality would be my pre-occupation for the future. Another idea crossed my mind as I wondered why men and women never mated in public like the cows, dogs, hens and goats.

Although in Kenya petting and kissing in public still raised eye-brows, the miniskirts had come and gone. Now there were the slits in the skirts to expose female legs. We definitely were getting somewhere in the direction of openness as far as sex and morality were concerned.

I had read in Desmond Morris book 'The Naked Ape' that our brain was too powerful an organ to allow men and women to rival openly over sex matters. This is what consequently led to monogamous relationships and the age categorisations in choice of sex partners. It also dictated against mother-sons, father-daughters and brothers-sisters, mating. But it still did not explain the secrecy that shrouded the things that all of us did, or craved to do, every other day — copulating with someone.

I was allocated one of the Registrars' flats number B10, on the ground floor, which had a car-park, kitchen, water-closet, bathroom, fairly large living room with a fire place and a spacious bed-room. This was to shelter me for the next two years. My previous accommodation in Woodley Kibera and Eastleigh were all very different from this. The Woodley Kibera bedsitter, was everything for me — my kitchen, bathroom, living room and bed-room. Only the Indian-type communal toilet was outside. The Eastleigh residence had a kitchen-cum-living-room, one bedroom and a permanently stinking and filthy toilet. Mary Nduku compared the place with a pigsty and it was therefore little wonder that she was delighted about the Registrars' flat B10 when she visited it.

"My house has no fireplace. We can now light a fire," she exclaimed as she spread her legs and straightened her back, producing loud creaks out of my ageing sofa.

"You'll break my sofa," I admonished.

"You should buy a new one!" she complained producing more squeaks with it.

"I am sure Mr. Brown has a magnificent fire place," I taunted, evoking a subject I used whenever I wanted a distance between me and Mary Nduku. I had spent the whole day on Neurosyphilis, a quite exhausting subject only to be visited by Nduku who at times burdened me with nagging proposals. Besides, I was expecting Mumbi, Dr GG's daughter, who had expressed great interest in seeing the Registrars' flats when I told her I had acquired one.

They were called Registrars' because this was where most post-graduate students (doctors) lived, running KCH under the supervision of the Senior doctors - surgeons, physicians and other specialists. The responsibility for clinical tests, consultations, minor surgery, prescriptions on most obstetrical, orthopaedic and paediatrics rested with, the registrars. The older doctors supervised and administered us while they also ran many clinics scattered all over the city. When major surgical and more complicated issues arose, we referred them to Dr Gichinga's type. This worked fairly well and we did not complain, but the existence of such clinics did at times earn government wrath because they robbed it (government) of most of its experts, besides providing vehicles for losses of its stores and medicines.

*　*　*

"This calls for a celebration. A flat with all the modern facilities," Nduku exclaimed ignoring my allusion to her white lover. "We should go to the Serena."

"I am not celebrating today," I grumpily said. I was in neither the mood to be with Nduku nor the inclination for the Serena. My purse could not even allow me to take Nduku into the Serena where her drinks cost all my booze-budget for a week.

"We can go to *masandukuni* then." *Masandukuni* were the cheap off-licensed drinking parlours named after the early wooden beer-crates often used as seats in such bars.

"I have had a really rough day."

"What is the matter Yosevu?"

"Nothing is the matter, only tired."

"Oh! tired of me, are you?"

"No, tired of everything." The discussion was taking us nowhere and I was getting terribly impatient. The time was now six o'clock and Mumbi was due in, any time, unless she had lost the direction. "Look, Nduku, why don't we celebrate another day, say tomorrow when I am feeling in the mood. In the meantime, I do not mind the rich lover-boy taking you to the Serena." The mention of Ian Brown's riches always produced defiance in Nduku.

"No, he'll take me to the Hilton tonight. I think I should even ring him right away," she said with venom and jumped to pick the telephone.

"That is an internal telephone, it never gets out of KCH" I told a half-truth because if one wanted to ring outside, one could use the KCH telephone operators.

She was offended by my mention of Ian Brown whom she treasured I now knew, for pecuniary reasons. She had argued on how nice the man was and how he in a way assisted me in that I could not afford to clothe her the way Ian Brown did. To Mary Nduku all the perfumes, nail polish, mascara and lip-sticks that came from Paris and her shoes, intimate apparel and dresses that were brought by Ian Brown from London, were blessings I should be grateful to the banker for. I did not accept her logic but she insisted that a doctor of my status required the company of exquisitely dressed women. This could have been true but for this particular Friday, I required a more ordinary person in the form of Dr GG's daughter. I bade Mary Nduku farewell then jumped on my bed to scheme my evening with Mumbi.

I was awaken by a loud knock on my door. It must have been some minutes after seven o'clock, when Mumbi finally made it to registrars' flat number, B10. She wore some blue denim jeans that emphasized her slim beautiful form, a yellow blouse and a red neck scarf that made her look like an American film star. Her stilettoes were black, unmistakably the superior, imported type that Nduku would brag about.

"So this is where dad said super doctors are made," she screamed sitting herself on the old sofa and kicking her shoes off.

"Yes, this is the registrars' village."

"You'll be here for a year."

"No, for two years."

"That means you won't marry until 1980."

"It does not mean that. I can marry any time — tomorrow, 1980, 1990, the year 2000 ..."

"I will not marry here."

I was about to tell her that I was not contemplating marrying anyone yet, when something warned me against it. I gave Mumbi my photo album to study, asked her to feel free with the fridge in which I had stocked Pilsners. After a bath, I dressed in jeans then took her to the *masandukuni* opposite the old Kenya Police Dogs' Station. This was within a walking distance of KCH and was most popular with us not only because of its closeness to us but also because it sold beer very cheaply. The fact that they served no wines, liquors or spirits, which were fairly costly items in the country, saved us of Mary Nduku's types who had no mercy with men's purses.

The canteen was crowded and I recognized several registrars, nurses and clinical assistants flushing their day's thirst away with Tuskers, Pilsners and White Caps. There was a lot of agitated talk all over the place and groups had formed in different corners. We sat on the empty bench next to the juke box and I ordered four White Caps and four Pilsners that I hoped would see us through most of the evening. We started taking our drinks that Mumbi this time appeared quite capable of swallowing.

"I haven't had a drink for a week," she explained. "I had a running stomach most of the week."

"How is Mombasa?"

"Oh, the usual. The American sailors have now gone."

"What do you mean?"

"Have you not heard of the American marine's season?"

"No, I haven't."

"Well, it is a time when the whole of Mombasa, harvests dollars, yens and even pounds from the visit of American sailors, heavy giants who drink, spend and take a lot of women."

"Oh!" I exclaimed finding this discourse rather interesting.

"House-wives leave home and masquerade like us single girls, invade the Florida, Casablanca and most beach hotels in search of the American sailors."

"Do you?"

"I said everyone, even some men do," she said flatly, but I did not want to press the subject further. I discovered I did not know much about Mumbi besides that she was born in 1957, had schooled up to form 4 out of which she had come out with a third division grade, school certificate. She had gone to Mombasa for a secretarial course which she flopped in.

"The typewriter is still a very ghastly instrument," she had said. "Every time, I see one, I squirm."

"What do you plan to do for a career?" I asked avoiding the issue of what she currently did.

"Well, to get married and get ten kids."

"So many?"

"A doctor's salary and free medicines, is all I need."

"I see."

Mumbi had no doubts about what fate had in store for her, she was to marry a doctor richer than her father, would be extremely faithful to him, even if she knew men were infidels and bear him ten kids. In the meantime she was reaping all there was to get from Mombasa.

"I have two more years, is that it?" she started on the subject I dreaded once more.

"Yes," I said simply not knowing that I was driving a nail into my own coffin.

We continued drinking and as the hours crawled towards ten o'clock I overheard a conversation that made me shudder.

"Can you imagine he never set foot on Kisumu, since the killing of Tom," a tall Luo clinical assistant, I recognised, said.

"All the same, save for the dominance of his Kikuyu tribe, he was a good leader," the doctor added and I became more alert.

"What are the people talking about?" I asked Mumbi.

"They are discussing Kenyatta's death."

"Kenyatta's what?" It was as if I had been struck a fast blow.

"Where have you been the whole day? They began broadcasting it since one o'clock this afternoon."

I had not heard that the old man who had ruled Kenya for fifteen years or so, had died. Mumbi told me of how a few days before he had called all members of his family to Mombasa and all the members of the diplomatic corps abroad and how the events of the week had proven the view that he (Kenyatta), knew he was going.

"A lot of people who die of natural causes, can tell when they are due," I told Mumbi, then noticed that all the groups in the "Dog-section" canteen as this place was called, were freely discussing the Twenty Second August, 1978, event.

"I am glad neither Koinange nor Gichuru have taken over. These people are dangerous," a slim looking man who talked with a Kamba accent asserted.

"Let us hope Moi will bring about a better tribal balance in government and economic conditions."

"You think they'll let him rule?"

"Why not? Whom can they field? Gichuru will not let Koinange nor will Koinange let Gichuru."

I dared not join in the political discussions. My present pre-occupation was how I would contribute to Kenya through saving it from all venereal diseases. I recalled my mother, four years ago having charged that we doctors wanted more syphilis, gonorrhoea and herpes as they kept us employed. I had since come to realize that existence of diseases or not, most doctors loved people, fully believed in healthy bodies and would love a utopian disease free world even if they made them redundant. Only a few such as Dr Gichinga probably would be tempted to abet an unhealthy world where their clinics continued draining the sick of their savings.

The "Dog-Section" canteen closed at eleven although most of the days it used to open until the last customer was out, which was often as late as four or five. I drunkenly walked Mumbi home through the two gates that ensured trespassers do not stray into the hospital. We found the watchmen asleep and Mumbi had to bang their pen with her right shoe repeatedly, for them to wake up and let us in.

"Which flat?" the elderly watchman clad in a black thick army rain-coat, asked.

"B10, I've just moved in," I told him then yawned to emphasize the fact that I needed a well-earned sleep. We were let in and went straight to bed, without bothering to grab anything for a bite.

We must have made love in a manner that Mumbi did not approve, because with hindsight I recalled her shoving my body off her and calling me a sleepy sot. Then I woke up thinking I was dreaming. Some extremely loud thuds were being made on my front door.

"Yosevu, Yosevu, Dr Munguti, wake up," I recognized Nduku's hysterical voice and peeping through the key-hole I recognized her pinkish Peugeot.

"Just hold on," I shouted, then grabbed a towel, put it around my loins then opened the door hoping not to awake Mumbi.

"What is the matter?" I asked her, reluctant to invite her into my house at this late hour.

"I am freezing," she swore, then pushed me out of the doorway. She made as if to walk into the bed-room and I found myself unconsciously grabbing her left hand and pulling her towards me.

"No. You are not going in there," I pleaded hoping I could conceal why she was not to enter my bed-room. She pulled off her hand with some agility and strength I had not known she had, cursed, then walked into my bed-room.

Although I had heard of group sex encounters before and once had shared a room with a college-mate in which we slept with two Ibadan prostitutes, I was quite unprepared for two girl friends in registrars' flat number, B10.

"Oh, what do we have here? Is this why you were barring me from entering?" she mocked, then pulled the blanket off Mumbi's face. Mumbi woke up, and struggled to open her eyelids, dazzled by the light.

"What the hell is this Dr Munguti?" she screamed pulling the sheet to cover her pointed nipples. It was at that moment I noticed the difference between the two women. Mumbi had sharp and long breasts and a flat belly, while Nduku had very large breasts, fatter body and some bulging of the stomach. In my confusion I noted that all I had read in medical schools had no practical application until issues such as those of having two females under one roof, confronted me.

"Nduku, we are extremely sleepy," I said and threw myself on the bed, which creaked as if protesting over the intrusion by Nduku."

"So am I," she said pulling the blankets and joining us on the bed without removing her clothes. The bed creaked even more under the weight of three adults. Mary's belt poked on my back and I cursed telling her to remove it if she wanted to sleep. She removed her clothes and I found myself sandwiched between two women whom I had intimate knowledge of.

After about half an hour Mumbi realised I was uncomfortable.

"Go ahead with her. I've had my share," she grumpily said turning her back towards me. "We call it a twosome in Mombasa." I pretended to be asleep and held on my guns, although I entertained the idea of this twosome. I could not sleep and when Nduku began fondling me, I succumbed to bodily urges. Both of them ingratiated me quite willingly for persons who had began the evening as rivals.

Nduku left very early in the morning asking me to enjoy the new find. I felt no guilt because I as yet belonged to no-one. Mary Nduku had his Ian Brown while Mumbi had the Mombasa studs that she so much talked about. The reference to the twosome in Mombasa however disturbed me and made me curious to know what Mumbi actually did in Mombasa for a living. I would bring the subject at the earliest convenience, I promised myself.

* * *

I looked at the clock that stood at my bookshelf next to my bed and saw that the time was half past seven. Mumbi slept peacefully, snoring slightly and I was tempted to wake her up. My head hurt out of all those nights' beers and sleeplessness and I wondered if I could absorb anything in class.

I jumped out of bed, heaved my body to the shower and opened it full throttle hoping the water-whipping would sober and awaken me up. It was when the water hit my back that I realized, I did not have classes till in the afternoon. I was, however, required to be on call in my room. I turned off my shower, wiped the water that had dripped on my back, then went back to bed.

"That was a wonderful night." Mumbi had woken up.

"What?"

"I said that was wonderful."

"I still do not understand."

"You were a wonderful lover last night."

"Was, I?"

"Yes, twosomes brings the animal instinct in all of us and we do it far better than normal."

"How do you know?"

"What do you think I do in Mombasa? The sailors are particularly fond of them." Mumbi should as well have struck me like lightning.

"So you move with American sailors?" I asked the obvious question.

"Yes, Americans, Koreans, Pakistanis, Japanese and even Singaporean sailors. They are more generous than the local boys," she said flatly and with all the candour she could master.

"What do you do for a living?" I had to know the whole bitter truth.

"Nothing really. Make myself beautiful during the day, entertain the sailors when they are in town and live."

86

"You mean you sell your body like a prostitute?"

"Don't all women sell their bodies?"

"Not all."

"Are you sure?"

"Yes."

"Last night you bought me, didn't you?"

"I did not."

"And the day we were in Nderu?"

"I did not."

"You must be blind. I drunk ten Pilsners off you at Nderu. Last night, some seven. In addition I slept on your bed and will drink your tea and eat your food ... ..."

"That is not buying."

"What about the lady whom I shared you with? Who is she to drive a Peugeot 304, wear London-made shoes and clothes and possess the make-up of a Kenyan princess?"

"She is a secretary."

"Who never sells her body?"

"I do not know."

"Where does one draw a line between selling and giving it free anyway?"

"I want to go to sleep." I gave up on Mumbi's cross-examination. She had, I had to admit, a witty mind that appeared full of justification for whatever challenges were made to her. I had to admit some of the things she said about prostitution were patently true.

I must have fallen asleep because when I woke up the sun was fully shining and the clock indicated eleven. Mumbi was all gone leaving her knickers and brassiere hanging on my bathroom towels' rest. My head was now clearer although I had fairly disturbing thoughts running around my head. I showered, dressed in my khaki working Kaunda suit, put on my white dust-coat with the red mandatory label indicating I was "Dr Munguti," then walked dangling my stethoscope towards Ward Twenty. Although Ward Twenty was not my duty ward any more, I visited Irene there whenever I had disturbing thoughts. Irene had become fairly privy to a lot of things that happened to me for I found her extremely understanding.

"Sister Irene, how are you?" She had become in addition to a hospital sister so close to me that I also regarded her as almost having a filial relationship with me.

"Okay Dr Munguti, and you?"

"I have slept with a prostitute."

"Oh! and you are sick."

"Oh! no."

"There is nothing wrong with that, unless she scarred you the way Leonard did to me." I was surprised she recalled an event that had taken place nearly four years ago.

"No, but the problem is, I was not aware of her profession." I went on to tell her of the little I knew of Dr GG's daughter and how I had considered her such a nice girl. With the revelation of her trade, I could hardly mix with American, Korean and Singaporean sailors in her world.

"Poor Dr Munguti, you are such a nice man." These were the type of exclamations that had developed between Irene and I. They apparently seemed to have mutual healing and soothing power. Whenever they were exchanged, all our tribulations appeared to ooze out. I have come to believe, that this is all I needed to hear from her and I would be back to normal. I thanked her and left for the canteen.

I flipped open my fly, to answer to the morning nature call. At first I hesitated not quite sure of the feeling. A moment later and there was no doubts about it. The characteristic burning was there striking me with unmistakable pain. I had gonorrhoea about five years before, during my college days at Ibadan. We even bragged in those days that one was not a man before he had circumcised the urethra. However the present attack was different because I had come to believe that as a nice man who never moved with prostitutes and only dated nice girls, I could not contact VD.

My medical obligations required that when I report to my doctor, I bring along my cohorts for treatment. My present ailment either involved Nduku or Mumbi. Worse still, even if one of them had been free of the disease, I must have acted as the transmitter between them and they were both now most probably infected. I had to move fast before Mumbi left for Mombasa.

I drove in my Ford Escort, KML 721, fairy fast and arrived at Nderu in thirty minutes. Dr GG was sober unlike other days although one could tell he had a rough night before.

"Yes Dr Munguti? These days you have forgotten Nderu eh?"

"No Dr GG I will never forget Nderu."

"Come in, this is a pleasant surprise."

"Congratulations, Mumbi told me you are now a registrar and that you even drive."

"Yes, Dr GG" I began sweating profusely at the mention of his daughter. I did not know that she could discuss about me with her father so freely, now that we had something to hide.

"Are you all right?" the old man asked touching my forehead and inspecting if I had a fever. "You know, the old Kikuyu saying, that a barber cannot barb the back of his neck?"

"I know the saying, that is why I have come to see you, I think it is gonorrhoea."

"Oh! Dr Munguti, you mean gonorrhoea could make you sweat like this? In Korea, Burma and even Somalia during the war, every time one hit the flesh, You had it. Drop those trousers."

I obeyed the old man who gave me some particularly painful injections on each buttock, then handed me half a tin of ampicillin which he swore would see me as fit as a fiddle in the next few days.

I did not inquire on Mumbi although her having mentioned that I had been with her, worried me. What would Dr GG feel if he knew, I wondered, that his daughter would have infected me with VD.

"This was all that was left after treating my daughter." I could have hit the roof! So the old man knew that the disease I had visited him for, had something to do with Mumbi, the daughter he loved so dearly. We never talked of the matter again.

As I drove back home, I felt great shame at what had happened. The Neisseria organisms must have come from Mumbi, I thought as I contemplated of my previously healthy genitals. The events of my last encounter with a female, however, became clearer that Nduku had been at the scene also, besides Mumbi!"

"Oh God!" I cursed aloud. "What have you done Dr Munguti, the Medical post-graduate class Pharisee?" Only the previous day I had strongly supported the case of condoms' vending machines being placed in *Majengo* public toilets if we were to win the war on the VDs menace. "Dr Joseph Munguti, not only were you reckless with your body but acted like a rat, an Anopheles mosquito or any other dangerous vector to two women!" I shouted at myself and hoped that it would never happen again. I would preach and practice the use of condoms to the letter.

* * *

Nduku entered my flat fuming. This was ten days after they had their twosome and a week after I had been doctored by Dr GG. She threw a three hundreds shillings bill at me swearing some unprintable expletive.

"Yosevu, you are dirty aren't you?"

"Oh! why?"

"You have given me VD."

"Nduku listen ... ..."

"I want a refund of my three hundred shillings first."

"For what?"

"See for yourself, my doctor says I have gonorrhoea from you."

"How does he figure it is me?"

"I am going go sue you, Yosevu."

I was not worried by either her threats of suing me or her asking me to refund some three hundred shillings. It was her accusing finger that was particularly irritating.

"But you flirt around with your *mzungu* lover, don't you?" I began a subject she was loathe to discuss.

"White men have no VD."

"What are you talking about?"

"Mr. Brown is nice, he does not go with prostitutes."

"How would you know when VD is white or black?"

We began an endless argument. I tried to prove to her how futile it would be for any of us to point accusing fingers at each other. How I thought it was her who had infected me with the VD and if it was not her, it would be nobody else.

"Yes, the Mombasa harlot?" she screamed, rose from the sofa that creaked whenever she sat or woke out of it, then jumped to the bed-room. "She should never keep her VD infected clothes here!" Nduku said.

Before I knew it, she had removed Mumbi's pants, brassiere and a dress, Eunice had left behind and threw them into the fire.

"No, Nduku don't, I pleaded with her but it was too late. The silken material had begun shrivelling and by the time I removed them out of the fire, some three, impossible-to-mend holes, had gone through Eunice's dress and Mumbi's clothes were half burnt.

* * *

One day I began comparing Nduku and Mumbi. I found to my horror that I was more drawn towards Mumbi the prostitute than Nduku, the secretary. Nduku was selfish, egocentric and a nag. Her world was all that mattered. Mumbi on the other hand was simple, loving, intelligent and never nagged me. She had said that in her strange way, she loved me. Nduku did not love me. I think she loved Ian Brown and his money. I found Mumbi terribly attractive and very good company to be with whether in or outside the bed. Nduku was on the other hand a pain in the wrong places. She dressed regally, perfumed herself ostensibly, but she was vile and vain. She expected too much out of me, whether material or spiritual and there was nothing I did well. The strange thing is that her taunts and nagging had an effect on me. I had even started dressing richly to match her and was now seeing age in my furniture. A craving for riches started creeping into me also, any time I thought of Brown's money.

One day I was in the deep of these thoughts when Eunice knocked at the door. She had left her car at the Nairobi Club of which she was a member and then walked to the Registrars' flats a few hundred metres to the south.

I explained the burning of her dress, which she took calmly but warned me about moving with simple women who directed their wrath at inanimate objects such as clothes rather than where such anger belonged. She was extremely understanding. She said she loved me and hoped one day I would realise this, to which I did not reply.

My love belonged elsewhere but I didn't know where. It was neither with Mumbi, Nduku nor Maimba's wife. It did not belong to Irene either because she was a sister to me — the only person who had a ready shoulder for me to cry on. Poor Irene, she was

92

so devoted to the things she did, unselfish, contented in life; happy with her father's love and my friendship and yet suffering for unfulfilled sexual urges for reasons she could not understand. Unbelievable.

* * *

Six months after entering KCH as a registrar, Gilbert died. There was a subtle celebration amongst the nurses and doctors who had suffered helplessly looking after him. Dr Gichinga was on duty in Ward Twenty and apparently the malady that Gilbert had braved for four and a half years finally caught up with him. Because of his views on euthanasia, abortion and heresies with regards to the hippocratic oath, the Central Hospital Board suspected foul play over Gilbert. Dr Gichinga was suspended but later re-instated when investigations failed to prove anything against him. He told me, that the period of this suspension, was the happiest of his life for he re-lived his medical days while manning the River Road Clinic. Since joining the registrars at KCH, I had been unable to work for Dr Gichinga although I had promised, I would.

Irene was convinced that Dr Gichinga poisoned Gilbert because when she left the ward the day he died, he had been extremely jovial and healthy. Irene claimed he had rolled his eyes and smiled at her, the smile she loved because of its special warmth and appreciation. She cried for several days after Gilbert was buried at the Langata Cemetery.

Eunice prevailed upon me that we visit Tala Inn. I had sworn never to go to Tala in a *matatu*. My junkish KML 721, Ford Escort, was parked in my flat at the Registrars' village. I therefore saw no breach of the covenant that I would never go to Tala in a *matatu*, if I agreed to drive in Eunice's BMW 320.

We left on a Friday evening and entered Tala around 7.00 p.m. As we approached the town, fears of being seen with a sugar mummy assailed me. What would my mother think if she saw me with a lady nearly her age? I wondered, shuddering at the thought. Although Eunice was about ten years younger than my mother, her eleven years seniority to me, made her appear like a mother to me. She was a nice lady, very devoted to me, for reasons best known to herself. I was, however, getting concerned about the frequency of her visits. We had began with Friday evening visits till 10.00 p.m. during which we, as a rule, slept for three hours. Later on, it became overnight stays on Friday evenings. A few weeks later, Fridays and Saturdays. Then one day, she started breaking the week with a Wednesday visit. It was then that I realised that she was exhausting me. I noticed that whenever she appeared on the Registrars' flat B 10, I would cringe inside and make the silent wail of "Oh no, not again! ... ."

I left her sitting in the BMW which she now allowed me to drive, recognizing that male chauvinism required that I, rather than she, drove the car. Although I preferred her sitting in the back seat, she insisted on the front one making me appear a driver to her rather than the owner of the car.

"Have you got a room?" I asked the reception clerk.

"Yes, a double room."

"How much."

"Sixty shillings."

I paid without hesitation although I knew this would betray me further was Eunice to be noticed inside the car. I then asked for three White Caps, one roast chicken and a bottle of the Towers wine that Eunice drank. I collected the keys and the drinks making sure the waiters did not visit us lest they saw my companion. Eunice was a lovely woman. Her plumpness and age, however, made her appear a mother rather than the nice Kamba girl my mother wished me to marry. We were in Tala and I could not let the word go around that I was behaving in an antithetical manner to my mother's life-time wish.

We slept in Room 21 of Tala Inn, locked away from the bar and the restaurant. I feared she would argue over wearing Durex condoms but she surprised me by adeptly helping me into them. In Nairobi the need to hide from persons that would recognize her as the financial giant's wife, made us hide at the Nice People's Rendezvous or some suburban boarding and lodging house. It always pained me that I was a fugitive in my own city hence my hatred for all the times we socialized in Nairobi. In Tala the tables seemed turned. She burnt with anger, I could see, as we ate our chicken penned in the Tala Inn room for apparently no understandable reason. This time she failed to realise, how "dangerous" it would be for anyone to recognise us. It would accelerate my mother's march towards the grave and I did not want to be the one responsible.

Our best times were in Kisumu, Nakuru and Kitale. In these towns sugar daddies, mummies, girls and sugar boys were accepted phenomena, a thing I have puzzled over, to this day.

In the morning Mrs. Maimba surprised me.

"I must see your mother?"

"What?"

"We cannot come to Tala and I do not see your mother."

Although I was terribly afraid of letting the cat out about my relationship with Eunice, I felt a great urge to visit my birth place.

"Indeed, yes, we cannot," I agreed with her.

My home was only two kilometres from Tala township towards Kangundo. It was a normal four acre peasant *shamba* from which we had obtained all our livelihood when growing up. There were four huts, one belonging to my mother (kitchen), my sisters' and brothers' huts and my father's which was corrugated iron-roofed, bigger and square unlike the other three that were round and grass-thatched. Saturdays were market days for Tala and we found our mother preparing to go and vend her *muthokoi*, the kamba name for pestle-pounded maize with the testa removed. It is a very popular food with us. The whole household moved out to see the visitors with a beautiful BMW 320 that was intruding into their peace.

"It is Yosevu!" my sister Betty, screamed.

"He now has a car!" my brother, Muteti, shouted.

"We thought you had been swallowed by the city and would never set foot on Tala again," my mother complained shaking my hand and that of Eunice, askance.

"She is our matron. Came to buy some gourds, cow peas and *muthokoi*," I explained, warding off the blow that my mother was sure to throw with regards to a non-Kamba woman in my life let alone an elderly one.

"Oh, thank you. Welcome to our humble home. I am glad you have come at the right moment. Your dad is not feeling very well but he may see you after you have rested," my mother advised as she led us to her kitchen and had us sit on her low stools next to the smoky three-stone fire that she cooked her meals over. Eunice was wonderful. She merged with my family extremely well, helping my mother cook her *muthokoi*, constantly pushing in the firewood and effectively blowing into the fire whenever the wood required re-kindling. I left them to their devices and went to see my grandfather who was reportedly doing his last days on earth. The old man slept on his hard wooden rafters' bed out of which he now could not move. My mother had carried out all that was required for his feeding (which now involved liquid food only) washing and even his ablutions.

"Is that you Munguti?" his weak voice came to which I answered in the affirmative.

"You've come to see me before I go?" he continued.

"You are not going grandpa."

"I am going. Come here for your blessings."

I obeyed grandpa although protesting that he was not going. He spat on my face, then spat into his chest, then commended me to his gods asking me to live an honest nice life. He died, I learnt later, that Saturday evening after we had returned to Nairobi.

Lunch was served in my father's hut. He, too, was askance when he met Eunice and I gave the same explanation about gourds, *muthokoi* and cow peas. I knew, however, they had not been completely convinced. Mrs. Maimba made matters worse when she bought all the *muthokoi* my mother had and gave each of them, (mum and dad) three hundred shillings. My parents took the rich lady's money. I cursed the gesture for it let out the secret about us, that I associated with a lady who could freely part with six hundred shillings, for apparently no good reason. We quarrelled over this money on our way to Nairobi because it had been produced as if it was a bridegroom price. Eunice protested that there was absolutely nothing wrong with her generosity to my parents. She did the same to hers and in her traditional setting in Banana Hill, no-one visited other people's homes empty-handed. Whenever we quarrelled, which was extremely rare, she drove me to the Nice People's Rendezvous, a lover's paradise in Pangani overlooking the Muthaiga River and Mathare Valley slums.

David Kambo had travelled extensively in the country in his younger days first as a bus conductor, then as a driver and later on as an inspector for the OTC, the bus company that Nairobians had nicknamed *Onyango twende choo* (Onyango let us go to the toilet) and which now had extensive services all over the republic. In his travels he had seen the craving by visitors for clean premises with clean toilets, bed-sheets, rooms and the eating/drinking halls. He developed an obsession for cleanliness and when he set up this joint he personally supervised the cleanliness in the rooms. This earned his boarding and lodging house fame for few lodgers were able to forget the spotlessness of the accommodation it offered. He discriminated (by claiming the house was full against the cheaply dressed Mathare and *Majengo* women who called to ask for accommodation for clients) then hiked the price for accommodation to bar the lower income groups. After this he closed the bar altogether. By 1978, the Rendezvous had become an exclusive lodging house for a siesta, overnight stay and even weekend honey-moon events.

By the time Eunice and I visited it, it was what could be described as a nuptial or coupling house. Men and women and, in particular middle-aged men with young women, visited the Rendezvous standing in pairs like in the Noah's Ark. They paid money at the counter, received a cake of soap, a towel and a key then proceeded without further explanations to their respective rooms.

In 1978, Kambo looked at his palace. He reflected on all the people who had patronised it - justices of the peace, permanent secretaries, bankers, house-wives, personal secretaries, registered nurses, headmasters, pilots, policemen, lawyers, Members of Parliament. All these people came for morning and afternoon sessions with their lovers. Others for overnight stays most of which ended at two or three in the morning so that the patrons returned to their spouses before dawn. He named it, "NICE PEOPLE'S RENDEZVOUS".

We had talked at length inside room eleven of the Nice People's Rendezvous. She had explained how neither she nor her husband, Maimba, had been born with silver spoons in their mouths. Banana Hill where she was born was poorer than Tala as most people had less than an acre of land to live on. For firewood they used maize cobs and stalks. To feed the family her father had to pull a hand-cart called *mkoko-teni* in Nairobi from morning till evening and her mother had to pick coffee or tea in the European farms around Banana Hill. She had obtained a Kenya African Secondary Education Certificate from Kabete, trained as a typist then rose to a secretary through extremely rigorous efforts of scrubbing floors, cleaning office toilets and making tea for Asian and European managers with the Union Bank of South Africa. It was there that she met Godfrey Maimba, then a bank clerk and they thought (her words) that they were in love.

"We have to be going back now," she said, getting out of bed and proceeding with the ritual of showering, powdering herself, applying her make-up. I preferred bathing in my flat and so, other than dabbing my sweat off with a towel, I put on my clothes and shoes then walked down the steps that would take me out of Eunice Maimba's clutches for a few days. We had just handed over the keys to the receptionist when I saw a familiar figure coming out of a black Mercedes 280, one of the few cars of the type in the country. He opened the door and let out a slim looking young lady, not very much older than Dr GG's daughter, Mumbi. Eunice Maimba saw him and let out a curse.

"So he also knows this place .....? And he has a lover in addition to my maid!" she said, looking at her husband. I could have fainted when I recognized Godfrey Maimba, however, Eunice held my arm firmly and walked me away. Her husband took the arm of the little girl, no doubt his daughter's age and pulled her in the opposite direction towards the reception desk. I was neither sure nor cared to know if he recognized us. All I felt was pity for men and women who believed that in all married relationships men and women lived in strict observance of the biblical statement that, "and the twain shall be one flesh and let no man put them asunder".

Wekesa found Irene and I at the "Dog's Section" Canteen where I had taken her to cool down after she poured her problems with her mother to me. On Friday afternoon, an old friend, one John Kimaru, who lived in Kitale had visited her at the hospital. They had decided to go to the Kikuyu Country Club disco. They had danced, eaten roasted goat meat and made merry with Tusker Exports and her favourite drink, Pilsner. John Kimaru had been very lavish, or so Irene thought, hiring a taxi all the way to Kikuyu from Nairobi and paying for everything they spent. At around one o'clock they had decided to hire a room and spend the night at the Country Club. At the reception desk they met her mother in the company of the man whose buttocks her father had stabbed while he made love to her mother. A quarrel had ensued with the mother accusing the daughter of being cheap and the daughter retorting that the mother was an infidel and immoral. Naomi had cursed her daughter calling her thick and narrow-minded like her father. She had asked her to telephone him if she dared and tell him (father) that his wife (mother) was having a very good time. Irene had come to understand that telling on her mother tormented her father much more than it hurt Naomi, hence her confusion on what to do.

"Does your father have a lover?"

"Oh! no," she half-shouted.

"I think he needs one," I said, simply believing that the only way to sort out unfaithfulness in marital relationships was to join the sinning multiple lovers.

"Dr Munguti, I have been looking for you?"

"Am I in trouble again Chief Inspector?" I asked Paul Wekesa whom I had come to like as an honest man who loved his job and did it well without any malice.

"It is about the X-ray machine that was in the River Road Clinic."

"What of it?"

"We would like to trace it?"

"It is in the clinic."

"No, it is not."

"Then you must ask Dr Waweru Gichinga. Why do you want it anyway?"

"We would like to check its serial number and a few things about its purchase."

"Oh!" I smelled a rat. I had all along wondered why the machine was kept with a bit of secrecy and recalled my employer talking of transferring it to another clinic he was starting in the Eastleigh area especially for theatrical and surgical purposes.

Wekesa outsmarted Dr Gichinga this time. They managed to trace the X-ray in his mother's *shamba*, buried in a banana plantation, together with several bottles of medicines, vials and medical stores and equipment, all bearing the incriminating label "KCH, GK". The trial was brief as Dr Gichinga accepted all the ten counts of "theft by servant". They put him in for four years on all counts, which amounted to imprisonment for forty years!

We, all friends and foes of Gichinga, felt sorry for him wondering how he would survive forty years in prison. Paul Wekesa, however explained that he would stay for only four years since the sentences of the ten offences were to run concurrently.

In December, I received a letter from Dr Gichinga with the Kamiti prison's clearance. He asked me to run the River Road Clinic as my own. He wanted no money but to see that the place was kept running while he was away. I had by now learnt that most of my colleagues joined private practitioners in town for *kibarua* as they called part-time employment, but those who were dishonest carried out consultations in the walls of the KCH. Stories were even filtering to me of drug shortages and lack of laboratory chemicals unless patients paid something to the medical staff. It was also a known secret that placement on beds for patients at times required bribes.

In Ibadan there was nothing peculiar about this. In Kenya however, the hospital authorities were quick to deny the existence of such things. The realities of developing economies with limited resources were, however as true as economists had postulated, that scarcity commanded price on any goods and services. KCH's medicines, prescriptions and consultations were not exempt from this age-old economics law.

I promised to re-open Dr Gichinga's clinic as soon as my exams were over. I even invited Irene to help (with pay).

"You seem to be inheriting from the devil," she quipped.

"Would you not, if he bequeathed something to you?"

"Not the devil."

The theoretical part of my course was over and I was now busy collecting data and writing a sub-thesis on "Kenyan morality and its effects on the epidemiology of Gonorrhoea and the *Treponematoses*". For this course, I took time visiting most of the known brothels and knocking-shops in Nairobi, Mombasa, Nakuru, Kisumu, Eldoret, Kitale, Nyeri and Nanyuki. The knocking-shops were mainly in the slummy, *Majengo-type* of areas such as Shabab in Nakuru, Mathare in Nairobi, Kihuga Square in Eldoret and Mwembe Tayari in Mombasa. To avoid being conspicuous, I would wear a cap, tattered jeans and sometimes an over-coat in the guise of an ordinary labouring folk of the town. I mixed with illegal beer drinkers and sellers, drank *changaa* and *busaa*, sometimes smoked bhang and entered the mud-houses that specialised in vending quickies and many boarding and lodging houses such as Wakorinu that harboured prostitutes in the guise of daily lodgers. They were all there, young and old. Kikuyus, Luos, Kalenjins, Masais, Luhyas, Kisiis, Kambas, Somalis, Bajunis, Giriamas; every member of the Kenyan tribe was represented in the oldest trade, prostitution. Even Indians and Europeans had flats in the Westlands and Parklands areas where the richer clients visited. It was at that time when the daily papers, the *Citizen*, *Yardstick* and the *City Times* began copying some American and English by advertising prostitution in the name of "Escorts". The government must have realized the camouflage of prostitution renamed "Escorting" and somehow put a stop to the advertisements. Prostitution in these towns, however, flourished with the tourists adding to the fuel and making towns like Nairobi,

Mombasa and Kisumu the promised land for many literate and illiterate, unemployed and underprivileged women of all ages, shapes and sizes.

Apparently not many people bothered protecting themselves against gonorrhoea and the treponematoses, although swallowing of anti-biotics like penicillin or tetracycline capsules was quite common among clients and prostitutes. A particularly popular sulphonamide called "suta" was sold in the streets in spite of police vigilance against the practice. Condoms were a rarity I noticed, mainly because of a "flesh on flesh" dogma generally held by many Kenyans with regards to sexual pleasure. The Nairobi City Council (NCC) kept its doors open to confessed prostitutes. These had easy access to medical care for VD unlike the other people for whom declaring both primary and secondary contacts was required. I needed to find out why there was such laxity in prevention against sexually transmitted diseases

I entered a house on Digo Road in Pumwani one afternoon where a young lady greeted me warmly and invited me into her room. A charcoal fire burnt at the corner where some food was cooking. It made the room really hot and uncomfortable. She had two beds, a big and tidy one next to a tiny window and a small, theatre-type one without sheets on which she sat and outstretched her right hand towards me, using the other to remove her knickers. In Ibadan things were a bit more modest because I do not recall money changing hands before the knickers or our clothes were out. I got a sudden chill although I had meant to go through the whole exercise using a Durex condom.

"Bring money. It is not for free," she shrieked.

"Wait a minute," I protested.

"Five shillings, you are wasting valuable time," she shouted.

"Please open the door," I pleaded and threw the five shillings on the bunk. She took the money, smiled, opened the door then cursed.

"Get out!" she said, pointed at the door and let me out. "Did you think it was for free?"

"Damn you," I shouted back when I knew I was out of danger and several of her *majengo* colleagues opened their doors to look at a client who appeared to break their peace.

"*Bwana*, you have no money?" one at a corner jeered.

"Yes, I have no money," I said walking fast into the main street where I knew I was safer. When I told a friend of my experience at Pumwani, he laughed and told me that worse incidents had happened to people in whore-houses. Whole wallets would disappear in group-rooms when clients would be covered with blankets, held lovingly and made to feel the greatest of studs while companions soundlessly entered, removed the wallets and walked away. Shoes, coats, watches and all types of valuables also disappeared! For many Kenyan prostitutes poverty was the over-riding factor and venereal diseases were not a strong enough deterrent. For the men, the sexual relationship away from their families offered some comfort even if temporary, in generally friendless towns.

The women did not like condoms in spite of the protection they offered against VDs. In particular, the prostitutes found them time wasting as they delayed the man's orgasm. Some claimed that if left in their vaginas, surgery would be required to remove them. But these did not appear convincing reasons to me. A better explanation probably was that since nature abhors artificiality, wearing of a condom when a man and woman want to be at their most intimate situation, was naturally repugnant. For the Kenyan prostitute it reminded her of the obvious that, here was a casual carnal relationship which she would rather not have been reminded of. In fact, as a rule, the women never volunteered, I came to learn, that the men put on condoms. "I have no disease," was ofen heard in the rooms when clients suggested wearing the sheath, or, "I go to the clinic for check-up every week." It would appear the Pope had few problems in the condom controversy in our world of prostitution.

In November 1979, I decided to visit Mombasa and although I did not let Mumbi know before-hand, I meant to see her. She had said that all the waiters of the Sunshine Day and Night Club knew where she could be found. Besides Mumbi I would call on an old Tala High friend whom I knew as Dr Wahome of the Coast Metropolitan Hospital. He had gone to Mombasa as soon as he graduated from Makerere in 1973 and had never left practice in Mombasa. He was now a high-ranking member of the Kenya Medical Association (KMA). He was widely travelled and an acclaimed medic in the country. He would be useful to talk to, about my future plans.

I had visited Mombasa only once before, as a high school student in Tala. Our history society had gone to see the Fort Jesus, Gede Ruins and other historical sites of our oldest towns. All I could remember of the visit was plenty of heat, black-clad women, long shirts called *Kanzu* and many light-coloured persons of Arab, Portuguese, Indian and African origin. I boarded the Akamba bus at 8.00 p.m. at the company's bus-stop near the *Citizen* newspapers headquarters. The journey on the beautiful newly opened tarmac road took us nine hours with a half hour break at Mtito Andei where the passengers took light meals. At five on that Thursday morning, we reached Mombasa and were welcomed by the tropical heat, very much like that of Ibadan. Unlike Nairobi, Mombasa never slept. Activities of people walking, drinking in pubs and drawing along their hand carts, never stopped.

We alighted at the Dockworkers Club in Tononoka, a 24-hour club which gave shelter to beer-drinking visitors to Mombasa. I entered the stuffy bar, my ruck-sack in one hand and ordered two White Caps for breakfast. I sat in a corner to plan my three-day stay in Mombasa whose Port and people were similar to Ibadan's. This was expected, I realized, of places with similar climate. The sweating, the fans, the fish-smell, coconut trees, yams, rice, bananas, everything was so reminiscent of my student days that I found myself back to the University College Hospital days of Professor Dambo. I began humming (though silently), "*The year is over, what have I done?*" I have got myself webbed by four women, one who was selling her body in this city — I thought, cursed then finished my beer.

It was now seven o'clock and the first job to do was to look for accommodation. Putting my ruck-sack on my back, I left the club and went to look for a place to board. After walking for half a kilometre an attractive building caught my eye. I read "Astra Hotel, best rates in town," boldly written on the modern looking, two-storey building and something pulled me towards it. The charges were sixty shillings for "self-contained" (rooms with shower and toilet) and forty for non-self-contained rooms. I chose the self-contained facility, paid for it and was given a boarding room at that incredible hour of seven o'clock. I needed rest before embarking on my search for Dr Wahome, Mumbi and collecting more material for my sub-thesis.

I woke up around eleven sweating profusely, showered, dressed in some old tennis shorts, long unused, rubber shoes and short-sleeved shirt last worn in Ibadan. I then rang the Coast Metropolitan Hospital and felt as if the hand of the Lord was taking care of me when Dr Wahome came on the line. I explained I was Joseph Munguti now, a Registrar at the KCH. I had just arrived in Mombasa and wished to meet, if possible, "long" Wahome, as we had known him in Tala High.

"Oh! Father Guy's Joseph, how are you?" Dr Wahome was called 'Long Wahome' because of being the tallest boy in our class. I had forgotten they had called me "Father Guy's boy" in Tala because of my close association with the Principal.

"Yes, let us meet at the Manor at six o'clock." The telephone went dead even before I had asked Dr Wahome where the Manor was but I remembered Wahome as a taciturn man but extremely humble and dedicated to his duties. He must have rang off and gone back to his patients.

I had six to seven hours to explore Mombasa and add to my knowledge of the oldest trade in the world. I already knew what to look for, small alleys in the slums where women sat idly - smoking, plaiting their hair or merely looking at the sky. Just behind the Astra Hotel, they were unmistakably there sitting in a row with their doors slightly ajar. I was about to raise my right leg to avoid stepping on a heavy-set elderly lady when my hand was held in a familiar fashion.

"You want some tea," she asked showing some blackened teeth.
"Yes, how much?" I asked.

"Come inside." I obeyed then entered a dark mud-house with a fairly clean bed for such a slum. Some incense was burning from a corner.

"It is only five shillings," she said then went on to remove the wrapper around her loins. I was tempted to proceed further instead of merely interviewing her, but I had not been prepared for the suddenness with which the encounter came. I sat on her bed, pulled out a five-shilling note from my shirt pocket and gave it to her. She went on to peel off her skirt.

"Do you have a condom?" I asked.

"I am not sick. Do you think I am?"

"No."

She arched her fat legs, pulled off her skirt and impatiently awaited my response. I was so far from home and something warned me against giving in to the temptation.

"I'll come tomorrow. Keep the five shillings for me," I said patting her back and putting on my most mollifying smile."

"You'll have to bring another five shillings."

"We'll see," I said and walked out.

I walked off that slum then hit the *Mwembe Tayari* area proper. The situation was similar to the one before - lines and lines of women of all shapes, sizes and colours with men entering and leaving their rooms after purchasing quickies.

I had a lunch of goat meat and rice in a small hotel called Lebanon, went back to the Astra at around three p.m., rested, inquired about the Manor then left for my rendezvous with Dr "Long" Wahome. He was the same serious but friendly man about whom I had often wondered if he had any ill feelings for anyone. He had grown older like all of us, plumper and a little bit more talkative. I found him far easier to discuss with than I had expected. We had drinks, were served chips and steak that he ordered and discussed our activities since leaving Tala. I told him about Ibadan, KCH, Nderu and River Road Clinic and my present research on the epidemiology of gonorrhoea and the treponematoses. He said he had left Makerere, gone to Oxford, Perth and had just returned from Canberra in Australia having taken small courses on the respiratory system diseases that he hoped to specialize in. We then went back to morality and sexually transmitted diseases.

Dr Wahome laughed uncontrollably when I complained about my treatment at Digo Road in Pumwani-*Majengo*.

"In Soho, London, I paid a pimp two pounds, who led me to a receptionist who demanded two more for herself, before being ushered into the lady who had been advertised as offering French lessons," Dr Wahome said, making me more eager to learn of the developed countries' experiences. "In Kalgoorlie, Western Australia, the prostitutes have never left the mining town, in spite of police harassment. They sit with lamps and opened doors in rooms and in rows very similar to our *Mwembe Tayari* here. When one asked for twenty five dollars for a ten-minute affair, my mental calculation recorded three hundred shillings! and I jumped out of the room." I nearly broke my ribs guffawing at Dr Wahome's leap from a whore-house in faraway Australia. He went on to relate about Amsterdam and Paris where in the former, half-dressed ladies sit coquettishly in see-through glass windows and in the latter, on lamp-posts very much like our Nairobi girls. He contended that there was nothing the capitalist societies could do about prostitution so long as sex offered a method of human exploitation. Movies, magazines such as Mayfair, the multi-million seller Playboy, dances, singing, all exploited a basic craving in human beings for sex. In Paris and London men paid millions to attend strip-tease shows and movies, bought nude picture cards and all sorts of gadgets for eroticism.

"And the more sex was purchased the more *Treponema pallidum, Neisseria gonorrhoea, Trichomonas vaginalis, Haemophilus ducreyi....*"

"And more *Herpes simplex, Mycoplasma hominis, Candida albicans....,*" Dr Wahome added and we both laughed. I went on to tell him of my thesis that openness in views of venereal diseases could help in fighting its spread.

"That has been done in England where the venereal disease regulation of 1916 instructed local health authorities to provide clinics for diagnosis and treatment of VD confidentially and freely," he said.

"I guess our special treatment clinic in Cross Road was established on similar lines," I suggested.

"Yes, but as usual in our society, it is laced with problems of inadequate medical supplies, leading to bribes if one wants proper care," Dr Wahome moaned.

"I would like to set up a really free clinic for venereal diseases," I confessed.

"How would you finance it?"

"Oh, donors - World Health Organization (WHO), International Union Against the Venereal Diseases and the Treponematoses (IVDT), the NCC and even the KMA."

"It is an interesting proposition but highly doubtful if it will find support. Moralists will fight it as encouraging promiscuity, some doctors will think it deprives them of lucrative business and even the NCC may see it as an unnecessary strain on its budget."

"But I will prove with my thesis that this is one way of saving costs for the nation in venereal diseases' abatement," I insisted.

"I wish you luck."

After this academic exercise, we went on to further experiences. Dr Wahome had been married for now six years. He had two daughters and a loving wife but his secretary had made serious in-roads into their lives and she was now a type of co-wife for him.

"I am bringing her (secretary) to Nairobi in December to save me from your Florida girls," he laughed and I immediately placed him in the group of Mr. Maimba's type who were only slightly polygamous rather than promiscuous. I mentioned to him I was as yet unmarried but had two fairly steady relationships with a Mombasa lady and a Nairobi secretary. He reminded me of an old song about a travelling man who had a lovely girl in every town. We hummed it together after which he asserted that this was no longer necessary. In Sri Lanka on his way to Australia, he had been driven into the outskirts of the main city (because prostitution was strictly forbidden in the city centre) and literally found pens of women herded by men who brought them in a group for potential clients. The clients select one or two of the women who show and lead them to beds. The herders keep a stop-watch and a bell, superintend the temporary nuptial events, receive payments and supervise the trade in human flesh.

It was getting late and Dr Wahome now appeared exhausted. He suggested taking me back to my hotel but I declined going to bed without seeing Mombasa in the night. I asked him, instead, to drop me off at the Sunshine Day and Night Club. He obliged, insisted on my taking a hundred shillings for my beer then dropped me at the Sunshine leaving me his home telephone number in case I ever needed to call him while in Mombasa.

I entered the Sunshine, paid forty shillings at the gate and walked up the one flight of stairs into the stuffy, noisy, kaleidoscopic lights typical of Kenyan night clubs.

I sat in a counter between two young women who were extensively made up with red lipstick, green mascara, red finger nails and the latest long-hair wigs that made them look more Asiatic than African. One wore a mini-skirt and smoked while the other was in blue jeans and an open-back blouse. I asked for two cold White Caps, indifferently sat myself on a tall stool, pulled out an SM and joined in the merriment of the Sunshine. I had stopped smoking since coming back to Kenya but whenever I entered night-clubs, the urge got re-kindled and I found myself purchasing the menthol cigarette called SM and sometimes nicknamed *Sina Mpenzi* (I have no lover) or *Sitaki Malaya* (I don't like prostitutes). I smoked SMs as I surveyed the inmates of the Sunshine and wondered whether it was a *mpenzi* I was declaring I did not have or a *malaya* I did not like.

In a corner, sitting on a single divan in the company of two men, a white and a black, I recognized the familiar slim figure of Dr GG's daughter clad in white. She sipped something in a wine-glass and held a cigarette with the other then continued to talk agitatedly to the man who appeared white. I turned my eyes away not sure whether it was the three I did not want to see or I not to be seen by them.

"Can I have a drink mister?" the girl in a mini-skirt asked.

"I have no money," I answered.

"And a cigarette?" the one in blue jeans added, taking my SM packet and removing a cigarette without waiting for my consent.

Although as a rule I never accepted such behaviour from strangers, I had a gut feeling that this was these women's territory and I had to go by theirs and not my rules.

"You are new here, aren't you?" the one who lit one of my cigarettes challenged.

"No, I am not."

"Where do you come from?"

"*Mwembe Tayari*." I was not liking either the company or the conversation. I was between the devil and the deep blue sea as I debated whether to interrupt Dr GG's daughter's company or stick with these girls pestering me.

"Waiter, a Pilsner and put it in his bill," the mini-skirt one ordered. I protested, took my glass and beer bottle then strode towards Dr GG's daughter's corner. She saw me, recognized me then strode to meet me, arms outstretched. It was a warm kiss and embrace and although remarkably welcoming, I felt embarrassed in front of all those people. Its sincerity, however, touched me.

"And how is lovely Mumbi?" I said.

"Very fine indeed and how is my husband?" she casually said, kissing me on the cheek once more.

"I am fine," I said then remembered I had nailed another one in my coffin.

"Come, I'll introduce you to these people," she said, as she pulled me to the corner where the white and black man sat sipping what must have been Vodka since a half-drank bottle stood majestically between them. "This is Major Oluoch and Captain Blackmann, meet my husband Dr Munguti." I shook hands with Captain Blackmann first, who stood at a towering six feet, then Major Oluoch, who was about five feet five. After this we sat down to exchange all sorts of information and life experiences. Captain Blackmann was from Helsinki, Finland and commanded a ship that had docked in Zanzibar from which he had flown to Mombasa to see the beautiful town he had left one year before. Major Oluoch was in the Kenya Navy and was a friend of "my wife" Mumbi.

"Someone has to take care of me when you are three hundred miles away." Dr GG's daughter laughed. "And the moment you ditch me, I'll be off to Helsinki. Is that not so Captain?"

"Yes, we shall sail in the *Kemi öy*," Captain Blackmann said, words that appeared quite serious. We drank, ate chicken meat and I noticed Mumbi particularly enjoying the attention of the three men. A tinge of jealousy touched me when Captain Blackmann pulled her close as they danced and she put her arms around his neck. I pinched myself warning myself that tables had now been turned and it was time I and the Captain had our twosome. Major Oluoch's turn with Mumbi came and he danced with her beautifully. I had never been to a dance for a long time and was quite apprehensive of my turn. At Ibadan we did the "highlife," a disorderly dance that required no special practice. Fortunately when my turn came, an old tune of a popular slow waltz was played by the Bongo Boys and, as if old Armstrong had awaken from the dead, the trumpets blared.

"We were waltzing together," the vocalist sang. "in the dreamy melody, when a stranger walked in and you walked away..." he continued and I added "Mumbi wa Gikere..."

I realized it was 2.00 a.m. and asked to be excused. Mumbi would not have it, we were all to leave together after Captain Blackmann and Major Oluoch had selected companions for the night.

"How about those girls at the corner, sea wolves?" she asked and beckoned the girls in the mini-skirt and blue jeans I had escaped from earlier.

"This is my husband, Dr Munguti," she introduced us. "Alice and Julia" she added. "Major Oluoch you know and this is my Captain Blackmann." Dr GG's daughter always amazed me with her honesty, carefree attitude and apparent peace with anything she did. She managed to pair off Captain Blackmann with Julia and Major Oluoch with Alice, warning them that the men had only been leased as they belonged to her.

"We can now go, Dr Joseph Munguti," she ordered and we left the Sunshine Day and Night Club feeling high with all that booze, dancing and noise. I told her that I had a room at the Astra which she ignored, called for a taxi and ordered the man to take her home. Apparently the taxi-driver was familiar with her home for he simply drove off once we got inside. I did not argue for I was curious to know where Dr GG's daughter lived. "Dr Munguti, you are going to enjoy a widow's mite, this time. It is all free so that in the future you at times think kindly of single girls," she teased as we drove out of Mombasa Island towards Malindi.

Her flat was on the second floor of a large stone building whose ground floor contained a shop, a bar, barber's-cum-hair saloon while the first floor was a bakery. The sweet smell of baked bread was quite welcoming as she opened her door and asked me to go in. It was quite a comfortable bed-sitter with all the facilities neatly set - a sink, an electric cooking stove, a small fridge, shower and toilet bowl all fitting in one room plus a large double bed, neatly set, which served also as a seat. On the two walls next to the bed, were full-length mirrors running along the bed and allowing full images of people in sleeping positions. I drank a glass of squash, peeled off my clothes and went to bed hoping to fall asleep as soon as I touched the pillow and sheets. Mumbi went to the toilet bowl, jetted her urine rather loudly, removed her dress, knickers and shoes, the only clothes she had, then joined me in bed. It was when she kissed me that I recalled one of the puzzles I had come to clear in Mombasa. "Mumbi, you recall the time we slept in my flat?" I began.

"Of course, I remember."

"I got sick."

"So did I. My dad had to inject me three times."

"What do you say about it?"

"Say what?"

"Infecting me with gonorrhoea."

"Infecting you with what?" she screamed, leapt out of bed and faced me like a cobra. She slapped me full in the face then began crying uncontrollably. "Dr Munguti, you are such a baby. I know gonorrhoea from the simplest of symptoms. I have never had it for years. With the exception of you, I have always insisted on new condoms!"

"I am sorry," I said, fully convinced she was telling the truth. The three-hundred-bill bearer must have been the culprit. We had a peaceful night and made love using some Chinese-made condoms and when I left Mombasa the following day, I knew that I loved Mumbi's sincerity in a strange way.

At last it was all over (or so I thought). The sub-thesis was typed, bound and submitted to Professor Oluoch, head of the Public Health Department and one retained by Dr Jim Byron of Obstetrics who supervised my project. I could now open the River Road Clinic as my consultancy work with KCH only required me part time.

A fortnight after submitting my sub-thesis I was called before the panel of examiners to make the oral defence of it (thesis); that we would gain tremendous progress in the fight against venereal diseases were we to provide by extensive and intensive media communications acceptance of sexually transmitted diseases instead of moralising about and concealing them.

The Chairman of the examiners was a Ghanaian, Dr Kwame Afrifa. Next to him was Mr. Aziz Asika from Nsukka University, Nigeria; Dr Paul Wood of Oxford University and Professor George Mbaluto, a Kenyan fellow tribesman who had migrated to Rhodesia and now taught at the University of Salisbury.

"Dr Munguti, you accept that venereal diseases have risen over the years because of greater mobility, continuing permissiveness, use of oral contraceptives more extensively and increasing promiscuity. Is this not acceptance of sexual freedoms and if so what mode of openness are you suggesting?" Professor Oluoch started.

"I have stated, sir, that all those are evolutionary processes in society without official (state) recognition and acceptance. Acceptance in providing free treatment, case-finding organizations and funds for fighting the disease," I said hoping I made the distinction between committed government action and lip-service, clear.

"Dr Munguti," Aziz Asika started. "You reject the view that prostitution is a major cause of venereal diseases and quote such communities as the Masai who do not practice prostitution within the traditional communities, female chimpanzees and baboons who avoid attack and collect male food while presenting themselves sexually and prostitutes who do not engage in coitus but masturbate clients, to support the view that the former cases are equally vulnerable to the spread of VD while with the latter (prostitutes) they can hardly receive venereal infection from their activities?"

"Yes?" I accepted not quite sure what this was leading to.

"But the researchers of prostitution are dealing with females without husbands who seek solutions to economic problems through coitus bartering - the slaves, captives, divorcees, widows, outcasts and the unmarriageable." Mr. Asika continued.

"Exactly, sir, I have stated that this is the bigotry that fuels the spread of VD; disadvantaging females from access to goods and services and, in particular medicine. I have looked at Russia, Finland, our traditional societies and current trends with licensing prostitution, provision of medical care to them specifically and condom usage. There is increasing evidence that it is the lack of medical care which increases the incidence of venereal diseases rather than sexual encounters per se."

"Dr Munguti," Paul Wood started. "How much is adequate medicine to a people? Every country is limited in what it can provide and has therefore to prioritise on health care."

"Exactly, sir. We give too little to venereal diseases epidemiology because of our moral stance that responsibility for venereal diseases lies elsewhere. All I am saying is that gonorrhoea, syphilis and chancroid should receive as much attention as the common cold."

"Dr Munguti," Professor Mbaluto started. "Why do you think the church is wrong when it condemns prostitution as an evil that fans the venereal diseases menace?"

"It is wrong because it does not recognize the inevitability of prostitution.   Venereal diseases are, after all, named after the Goddess Venus whose rules we all abide by whether in a brothel or through other arrangements."

My examiners burst out laughing at this although I did not think it was funny. Professor Kwame Afrifa summed up by saying that some countries had gone along with my proposals yet the diseases had not been eradicated. I answered that I was not aiming at eradication but at keeping them in tolerable levels.

* * *

Four months later and after the course was over, I received this together with the notification that I had passed my Master of Medicine examination in Venereology:

"Registrar University of Nairobi"
Re: Sub-thesis of Dr Joseph Munguti, Master of Medicine (Venereology) Candidate: Your Ref. 8050095 of May 1980

I have received Dr Munguti's sub-thesis entitled "Kenyan morality and its effects on the epidemiology of Gonorrhoea and the Treponematoses" and wish to report as follows:

The thesis of 66 pages (excluding references and appendices) is well written, demonstrating that the author has an excellent command of written English. There are only a couple of places where awkward usage occurs. It is remarkably free of spelling and typo errors. The organization is reasonably logical in moving from the general economy of Kenya to the specific situation of venereal diseases' medical care availability. However, the flow is not completely smooth and there is a certain amount of redundancy between sections and some chapters.

The aim of the study is stated at the end of the first chapter which centres on making medical care freely available for all Kenyans without moral or financial constraints which characterise a lot of venereal diseases' diagnosis and treatment

118

today. The case is built around a review of poverty orientated prostitution in Kenya today with a lot of rural-urban migration, unemployment, illiteracy, economic deprivation particularly for women and a booming tourism trade (both domestic and international). All this contributes to most venereal diseases spread which is exacerbated by moral and legal stands (by most Kenyans) against prostitution and venereal disease suffers even in such places as the special treatment clinic where the sick are otherwise entitled to free medical care.

I was disappointed that the author did not acknowledge that many developed economies have tried free access to medical care and that the moral constraints are part and parcel of society and are deep-rooted. They are best left to the churches, mosques and other religious forums.

Nevertheless I feel the quality of the argument is such that the convergence of evidence is convincing. Given the difficult nature of medical men dealing with moral and philosophical issues the deficiencies can be put down to inadequate time to complete the case. I therefore am willing to give the sub-thesis a (marginal) pass.

Yours sincerely,"

Although I passed and would be awarded my Master's degree in Medicine the examiner's review upset me. In all my academic career from the time I was in standard one, high school and even during my undergraduate studies at Ibadan, I had never scored mere pass marks. My grades were always credits and above and I was convinced that I should have scored better marks were it not for social prejudices against advocates of openness in sexual matters. I made a decision of using the River Road Clinic for vindicating my case. I re-opened it after two years' use by Wananchi Pharmacy as a store and placed a board in black-on-white bold letters that notified the clients of the clinic's specialization:

Dr. Joseph Munguti M.B., Ch.B (Ibadan), M. Med. (Nairobi).
VENEREOLOGIST.

The charges, I decided, were to be the bare minimum of twenty shillings for all venereal disease cases except for complicated ones that would be referred to the special treatment clinic or KCH. I wrote letters to the World Health Organization (WHO) and the NCC asking for moral and financial support in providing Nairobi with excellent venereal diseases' health care at extremely low rates. A month later I received a letter from the WHO noting my efforts and wishing me luck but regretting that it had no funds for venereal disease programmes at the moment. The NCC did not bother replying. However, after one month, I received a visit from the KMA officials who demanded an explanation for advertising private medical practice. I explained that I thought the people needed to know of the existence of such a special place and that the clinic was non-profit making. They disagreed with me and required the board be replaced by more moderate lettering. When I discussed with Nduku about my plans, she laughed, failing completely to understand whatever motivated me to such madness as offering free health care.

"Yosevu, you are courting martyrdom. Kenya is not Tanzania where they have outlawed private medical practice. You need to make as much money as possible in this country and only mad men will accept your views. Look at all the doctors and lawyers of Nairobi. They are all driving Mercedes, Jaguars and Volvos and you ....." she screamed like one demented.

"Please, Nduku, I have heard," I objected.

"All your friends are now living in Kitasuru, Lavington and Kileleshwa," she continued.

"I know, but this will come later. I have to save the medical profession of Kenya by fairer approaches to health care."

"Save it as who? What happened when you went on strike last year? Didn't the government accept private practice?"

"Yes, but not human exploitation."

"You are crazy, Dr Munguti and you will never make it!" she angrily said as she walked off, banging the door as she left. I was sorry for her. All she knew was making money even if this required being unethical.

I rejected Nduku's views. Money needed not change hands other than for costs of medicine, house rent, water and electricity and my doctor's pay. Profits belonged to businessmen of whom I was not. I was a doctor not a vendor of merchandise. If the owner of River Road Clinic thought otherwise, that was his problem and he had two more years to do in Kamiti Prison unless they gave him remission. The government decided against dual loyalty among us doctors.   We were either to serve our own clinics or the government hospitals. There was a bit of noise with consultants like myself still clinging to our private clinics while holding jobs with the KCH. I opted for the River Road Clinic for the two years I hoped to prove the point that patients were entitled to cheaper treatment for venereal diseases in particular and that the prevailing charges of 50, 100 and even 300 shillings, were immoral and exploitation of sex no better than that practiced in Soho and by the Harlem barons of New York in striptease clubs, pornographic films and magazines.

The River Road Clinic became very popular and I found myself working sometimes for ten to twelve hours. Contrary to what doctors who charged higher fees thought, in spite of the twenty shillings' treatment charges, the clinic never ran short of money. As much as one thousand shillings and more would be received on a daily basis. The clinic attracted all sorts of people who needed medical help — labourers, shop-stewards, barmaids, newspaper vendors, shoe-shine boys, men and women from all walks of life.

I asked Irene to assist during weekends, after work and during holidays and she became particularly helpful for injections and issuing of drugs while I concentrated on diagnosis and prescriptions. My policy was to make people realize that there was nothing to be ashamed of with regards to these diseases. How much I was contributing towards the eradication of gonorrhoea and syphilis, chancroid and trichomoniasis, I did not know, but I believed whole-heartedly that if all Kenyan doctors and hospitals had taken this attitude, the menace would be controlled.

One day, a reporter from the *City Times* called on me and asked if I minded an interview. I explained to him that it was against the rules of the KMA to advertise private clinics but he assured me that he was not advertising the clinic and he would make this absolutely clear in his report. He would merely echo my message that VD required sympathy and not ridicule. Four days after the reporter's visit, Mrs. Maimba called at the clinic. She showed me a newspaper article that called me Don Quixote in Nairobi medical circles. The article was fair in putting across my views but it did cast doubts on my capacity to deal with all cases of venereal diseases in Nairobi, let alone the whole country. There were VD sufferers who, for instance, the reporter rightly claimed, ran away from the name on my door, "Venereologist." Fear of being seen walking into a venereologist's clinic turned some people away! Otherwise the reporter decried the rising costs in private medical practice particularly as practiced by consultants.

A week after the *City Times* report, I was asked by a Voice of Kenya reporter to appear on TV to answer a few questions the public required to know about the River Road Clinic and my work. I advised that I could not appear on TV with regards to a private clinic but he brushed this off, explaining that I was appearing as Dr Joseph Munguti and not as the proprietor of The River Road clinic. It was my first TV appearance. The journalists from the *Yardstick*, *The Citizen* and *City Times* were all there.

They introduced themselves after the chairman had introduced the subject, then the volleys started, with the reporter from the *Yardstick* firing the first shot.

"Dr Munguti, why do you object to profits out of medicine while pharmacists, manufacturers of medical instruments and even funeral directors make money."

"Dr Livingstone, Dr Schweitzer and even Hippocrates himself never saw profits in ministering to the sick. Once you put profits in it, you give a half measure of prescriptions, time, skill and may even leave a sick person half-operated on. Any medical man knows the profit motive is an anathema in medical practice."

"The people you have quoted," the *Citizen* reporter said, "lived in non-monetary economies or at a time when one could afford philanthropy without economic gains. Today the Livingstones and Schweitzers of the world starve to death."

"I am not starving," I answered simply. "My girlfriend wants me to drive a Jaguar but that is a different matter." They all laughed.

"Dr Munguti," the chairman said, "you have been reported as a maverick doctor because everyone else charges two, three or even five times what you charge your VD patients; how do you manage?"

"I receive many patients; as many as fifty in a day. I guess the River Road Clinic commands what economists call economies of scale." I did not know I had offered someone my Achilles' heel to stab.

"So, Dr Munguti, you make your profits through economies of scale?" The *City Times* reporter asked, emphasizing "profits."

"I do not! The venereal disease sufferers are able to enjoy economies of scale in the medicines they pay for!" I said getting angry. All along I had believed I should be canonised for decrying profits, spending ten hours in the clinic and serving the nation's down-trodden and here was a reporter imputing the very motive I had rejected! I felt terribly insulted.

The interview was finally over. The chairman thanked me for a commendable job although he saw problems ahead particularly with regards to my incapacity to win the war alone. He was right. After this interview, hundreds of people began streaming into the clinic and in spite of changing the closing hours from seven to midnight, we could not cope. I got so exhausted that I began having doubts on the future of my work. The low costs I had advocated were now suffocating the clinic with an overwhelming number of patients only a big hospital could cope with. I had certainly mouthed more than I could chew.

Mrs. Maimba came to me complaining of rashes, itching and burning in her posterior. I examined her and discovered she had contracted trichomonas vaginalis. She said that other than I and her husband she did not indulge in sex with anyone else. I also told her that other than she and Nduku, I also was quite faithful.

"My husband has even forgotten making love to me."

"What do you mean?"

"I mean, he does not make love to me," she said.

"I thought you said it was only the two us."

"You make love to me. He forces me to offer the other area."

"Oh no."

"And I am now constantly having diarrhoea."

"You must refuse."

"I cannot, he'll throw me out of the house. He has become an animal these days; so terrible are the things he is doing to me."

The Penal Code contained prohibitions called unnatural acts and one of those so considered was sodomy. The Bajons, I had heard offered this area to husbands when menstruating as a matter of practice and in a lot of the literature on American sexual practices I had read, there was apparent acceptance for this form of sexual practice between willing men and women. The legal views of consenting adults on sodomy particularly when spouses were involved was a bit tricky and I saw no possibility of getting redress for Mrs. Maimba through police action. My job as a doctor also barred me from volunteering information to the police over this type of marital problem. I, however advised her to resist the treatment by whatever means not only because it induced diarrhoea, but also because of the possibility of other diseases like proctitis. I was sorry for Mrs. Maimba particularly since it appeared the husband had lost all love for her. He was now sodomising her in complete contempt not knowing that this could lead to far more serious problems for him and her.

24   1982

We were to vacate the Registrars' flats after graduating in July,
1982. Two bed-roomed flats befitting young consultants cost not
less than three thousand shillings in monthly rent if within close
proximity of the city centre. I mentioned that I was moving to Buru
Buru Estate in the Eastlands area where cheaper accommodation
could be found and Mary Nduku nearly puked.

"Yosevu, you are not a clerk, a clinical assistant or nurse. You
are now a consultant and must start behaving like one even in the
choice of where you live," she lectured. "Can't you see that even
us secretaries no longer want to be associated with the Eastlands
area?"

"What can I do? I do not as yet have money for Muthaiga,"
I protested.

"You can start with something middle-class such as Ngumo,
Nairobi West, Ngong Road or even Parklands," she insisted.

"Okay get something for me around the KCH that ranges
between two thousand and three thousand," I said, knowing she
would, for she was fairly well connected. She was, in a way right,
that as a professional with now eight years of service as a leading
venereologist, I needed accommodation similar to, if not better
than, the Registrars' flats.

After two days, she came up with a proposal I found fairly
attractive. I would share her three-bedroomed house and pay half
the rent. This worked out to two thousand shillings. I moved into
her house along Ngong Road on 15th July, 1982. She allocated me
one bedroom exclusively for my use, where I kept most of my
personal effects. The kitchen, bathroom, livingroom and the stores

were to be shared and although it was not part of the agreement we used Mary Nduku's bed most of the time. I provided for the food and the condoms. She did most of the cooking and for all practical purposes we set up a home.

On July 31st I took Nduku for a drink at the Zebra Hotel in Westlands, where we stayed until 12.00 midnight then drove back home.

Nduku woke me up around four to thunderous noise of shouting all over the city. Commotion reigned throughout the night until 6.00 a.m. when marshal music began playing in the radio and I knew something was amiss. At 6.30 a.m. the ill-fated announcement of a military takeover of the government came on the air. We were trapped in Ngong Road as we were made to understand that no vehicles were safe moving into the city centre. We stayed with the radio on throughout the day, locked up like everyone else, but to our relief the six o'clock news announced that the rebellion by a handful of disgruntled members of the Air Force had been crushed, the public were advised to keep calm, looting had to stop and the Government was in full control of the situation. On Monday morning, I decided to go to the clinic which had now become an obsession. On reaching the Uhuru Highway - Haile Selassie roundabout, I realized things were far from normal. We were ordered at gunpoint by security forces to turn back, which we did. It was not until a week was over when things calmed down that we could comfortably go to the city centre.

Although we had received reports of looting, rape and damage to shops all over the city, I had not imagined the magnitude of what I saw when I came to the city centre that Friday morning. Our whole street had its shops broken into and a lot of merchandise looted. Cartons, broken glass, steel grills, smashed doors, all sorts of garbage lay all over the street. My clinic was somehow spared as only a back window pane had been broken. The Wananchi Pharmacy was, however, looted and Patel's surgery was broken into. We therefore went into business as usual and I noticed that Irene had grown very fond of her work in the clinic although she confessed she had difficulties accepting prostitution and promiscuity. I advised her that for Kenya we were not dealing with simple cases of persons who preferred to be either prostitutes or promiscuous. They are, however, victims of a society that deprived them of a means of living hence making the women prostitutes. As for the promiscuous, they were victims of sex starvation away from their spouses in the rural areas whose answer to sexual needs were the quickies bartered at the various boarding and lodging houses mushrooming all over Nairobi.

* * *

I finished with one client with an advanced case of syphilis as evidenced by extensive psoriasiform rashes all over his genitals. I prescribed 2.4 mega-units of Benzathine penicillin, then asked him to go to the next room where injections and medicines were dispensed. Immediately the tall black man entered the nurse's room, I heard Irene scream. It was a strange twist of fate for when I rushed to the room, I found her holding a pair of scissors, dagger-wise and swearing that if the patient drew nearer, she was going to stab him.

"Dr Munguti, this is the beast who tortures women," she screamed.

"The what?"

"The Leonard pig!" she screamed. Then I recalled four years ago when a Mr. Leonard had allegedly brutalised Irene. So this was, I wondered, the six-foot giant who caused such a trauma in Irene that she no longer felt safe with men. I boiled inside but knew that vengeance belonged to the Lord particularly when medical care was involved.

"Please put the scissors down," I asked Irene as calmly as I could. "He'll not harm you this time," I advised then took over the nursing job which I knew Irene would not be capable of, for the day. Leonard had not said a thing as he appeared either confused or suffering from some mental disorder. All he did was to point at his genitals, roll his tongue like a hungry dog which had sighted food then mutter things I could not understand. I gave him two injections, one on each buttock, which he accepted without resistance. I asked him to come back in a week's time, but

128

he never appeared to understand. He did not return and I assumed he got cured of his malady.

I comforted Irene as much as I could, but I noticed that the sight of Leonard had brought back terrible memories long buried in her bosom. I would, I decided, talk to a psychotherapist about Irene and hope that she could come to terms with this event of years past.

*　*　*

My life with Mary Nduku lasted only two months. Sometimes we shared her car to go to work, for she never liked my inferior model, Ford Escort. I tried to emphasise that although we lived in the same house, we were independent in that I still had my life, unattached to anyone. I also emphasised that I would not interfere with her private life either. She began talking of wanting a baby but I made it quite clear that I did not want one as yet. In spite of this understanding, that we were simply sharing a house and a bed, Mary Nduku's baby-project became an obsession and I saw signs of her converting me to her stud. One night she complained that she could not stand condoms any longer and threatened to look for a more potent a lover than I. I repeated that I was not about to father her child and that she was free to others. She cursed, called me a Mombasa whore-monger and sugar-mummy's boy. I had thought my life with Mrs. Maimba a top secret but Mary Nduku's inference of a sugar-mummy in my life seemed to imply she knew.

"What do you mean?" I asked.

"I have seen you ten times with her in Nice People's Rendezvous," she challenged.

"What were you doing at the Nice People's Rendezvous?"

"I got sugar-daddies too."

"I thought you only had Ian Brown."

"Mr. Brown is not my lover, mine is a puisné judge," she said with pride.

"What is his name?"

129

"He is called *my Lord*," she mocked and I knew it was time we called off the discussion.

* * *

Three days after this discussion, I came home to find a Mercedes car parked next to Mary Nduku's Peugeot. Mr. "My Lord" was real and had made a visit, I thought, then parked my Ford Escort next to the blue Mercedes 250.

Two Securicor guards stood at the door and barred me from entering. I protested and said I could not be stopped from going into my house. They explained that they had orders from the owner of the house that I was not to be allowed in, as I had occupied it (his house) illegally.

"Which owner?" I asked furiously.

"The *mzungu*, he is inside," one of the guards said. At the mention of a *mzungu*, I grew mad and without waiting for further explanation, I pushed the bulky guard aside, opened the door and entered the living room.

"Where are you, Nduku?" I called out, but there was no reply. There were voices coming from her bedroom upstairs and something stopped me from venturing in there. Instead I listened to the agitated voices.

"You are behaving like a jealous African man," she challenged unmistakably sobbing.

"But I told you, I do not want him in my house," the English voice retorted. It sounded extremely calm and composed, I realized.

"He paid the house rent. He is therefore technically not a trespasser and if he has to go, I have to give him a quit notice." Mary Nduku apparently fully understood the Tenancy Act.

I could hold it no longer. Fishing a machete from the store, I climbed the stairs to confront my adversary. I had never seen Ian Brown before but from Mary Nduku's disclosures of him and the photographs she had, I was in no doubt when I faced his green eyes. He was tall, lean and had an extremely long nose.   He could not be described as handsome but he was certainly wealthy from the gold watch, gold-necklace, blue-black stripped suit and the shoes-to-match, that he wore.

"Can you people get out, now," I said furiously looking at Ian Brown full in the face.

"This is my house, Dr Munguti," Ian Brown protested and I detected a tinge of fear in his voice.

"Your house or not, get out before I kill you."

I think I could have cut him with the *panga* I held although I believed ordinarily I was a gentleman. My loathing for the man and his association with Nduku mixed with jealousy for his wealth, was choking me, I felt, as I stood there shaking furiously. He must have sensed danger because on hearing the words "kill you," he jerked like one receiving a whip then bolted out of the bedroom followed by Nduku. After this incident I could not continue living with Mary Nduku, but was lucky to get an equally comfortable flat at the Upper Hill region of Milimani. I paid a thousand shillings more in rent but this was an extremely fair price to pay for freedom from her and the likes of Ian Brown.

I told Irene I would accompany Dr GG and another man to pick up Dr Gichinga at the Kamiti Prison. She explained that she would leave the clinic once it reverted to the former owner because since the Gilbert murder, she could not afford to be anywhere near Dr Gichinga. I did not argue with her; she was going to carry to her grave the belief that Gichinga murdered Gilbert and since I knew nothing to vindicate the former, I preferred not to come to his defence. I had after all witnessed the death of the Tanzanian prostitute, Halima and I could not entirely vouch for Dr Gichinga's innocence.

Dr GG accompanied by a man he introduced as Kariuki the brother of Dr Gichinga, called at the clinic at 10.00 a.m. They explained that we needed to get to Kamiti before eleven so as not to keep a man in prison any longer than the four years he had served. I obliged and asked Irene to close as soon as the receptionist had tidied up the place and explain to him that the clinic would be closed for the rest of the day.

We arrived at the gates of Kamiti at 10.30 a.m. and explained that we had come to collect Dr Gichinga, a released prisoner. The gate sentry telephoned and was told that Dr Gichinga had been released and was awaiting collection. Being wary of prisons I left the formalities of receiving a human being from Kamiti to Dr GG and Dr Gichinga's brother. They left me seated in my Ford Escort as they walked towards the discharge office. I remained to brood over my next plans after Dr Gichinga returned. I knew I could not revert into a paid employee after two years of running the clinic on my own. I was however convinced that I should continue with my mission of providing cheap medical facilities to venereal disease sufferers. Even if I could not single-handedly eradicate venereal diseases from a city like Nairobi, the charges the victims were sometimes made to bear, were out of proportion to the cost, medicine, diagnosis and consultation required. The doctors I had talked to over this considered me stupid because, as they put it, it was not them who set the so-termed exorbitant fees. People were willing to be doctored under secrecy rather than visiting public clinics or such open ones as mine. In the posh areas of Nairobi within the walls of prestigious buildings where the common folk never walked, were places where the rich required their health care and for this they were prepared to pay. I was in the middle of these thoughts when I heard and noticed a man knocking on my window. I looked up and saw Dr GG, Mr. Kariuki and a man I presumed was Dr Gichinga. He had changed. Oh! I nearly screamed, what had they done to him? He appeared sixty like Dr GG, wizened and wrinkled. Whatever could have produced such features in a man within four years! I wondered.

"Hallo."

"Hallo ... why ... are ... you ... looking ... in ... such... horror?" he asked softly. "I haven't ... been ... on ... a ... honey ... moon ... you ... know. Take ... me ... home." His stammer had increased, I thought, looking at the once confident KCH consultant now reduced into a hesitant frightened old man.

"Where is home?" I asked.

"Lavington ... next ... to ... Kawangware ..." It was then that I realized, how little I knew about Dr Gichinga. I had worked with and for him for nearly four years and yet I had not met his wife or any of the four children they said he had. I did not know his home, friends or associates. All I knew was that he was terribly disgruntled with life and saw everything wrong with the KCH. I started the car as he begun narrating his experiences in prison. He had learnt carpentry and now knew a lot about timber, planing, nailing and dovetailing, he said. As for medicine his knowledge at it had gone completely stale as he had distanced himself from it in the four years he was in prison. They had once sent him to clean the local dispensary but he ended up with depression. Its origin was traced to the fact of his changing circumstances from an eminent consultant/surgeon to a cleaner. A few months in a proper hospital, Dr GG suggested, would sort out that staleness. Dr Gichinga would, however, not associate himself with the KCH again. I suggested he tried the Prince Kwan or Nairobi Hospital which took on specialist doctors.

We entered the city and Dr Gichinga asked me to drive into Lavington through Westlands to Austin Road up to the Convent Road. I had known this area during the internship days as our family doctors' practicals were conducted in Lavington although a lot of building constructions had sprung up since then.

"The house is at the junction of Convent Road and Loyangalani Drive," Dr Gichinga said. "I've heard the madam has started proceedings to divorce me and has taken possession of the house," he lamented.

"How can she take possession of your house," Dr GG demanded.

"Well, you know these things. I had it registered in her name like your Nderu Clinic because in the Civil Service you are not allowed private business or to own an estate without disclosing them ... Oh! we have arrived, straight to that black gate."

I drove to the gate then hooted. I observed the ominous signs of Lavington gates and read "*Mbwa kali*" and "Protected by wild guards", then blared the car horn once more. When no-one appeared to open the gate or respond, I, who was the youngest, felt obliged to do something about it. I pulled out of the car and came to the heavy steel gate. I tried to open it but it was securely fastened with heavy chain-link and an equally heavy Viro lock.

"Anyone in?" I shouted, hoping my voice would carry across the 500-metre space between the gate and the mansion which overlooked the Kawangware slums. There was no answer and Dr Gichinga became furious. He went for the car horn and started blaring it persistently. It worked although several heads of irate neighbours began popping out of windows to see who the hooligans intruding into the peace of Lavington were.

"There she is," Dr Gichinga, shouted as a lady in a night-dress and two girls aged about ten walked towards the gate. "Sarah, open the door," he commanded. On hearing her husband, the lady stood and started throwing curses at us.

"I told you, mad fellow, never to set foot in here. Go away you thief," she shouted at us, then to the children, "go hide children, the murderer is here!"

I had never witnessed such a spectacle. Dr Gichinga ran out of the car and in a blind frenzy scaled the steel door nearly crucifying himself on the spikes lining the top as he tried to jump into his compound. The children fled from him and as we pulled him from the gate his right hand badly cut, he began crying. "My children, my own flesh and blood running away from me! Sarah, I will kill you with these bare hands...," he swore.

We were attracting a crowd and I decided we would be safer out of there. We got back into the car and I drove fast back in the direction we had come. I told Dr Gichinga, who was protesting, that he would sort out his domestic problems after the hand was bandaged.

"Take me to a pub," Dr Gichinga ordered.

"Which one?" I asked.

"Any of the River Road ones."

"We'll go through the clinic to see to your hand first," I insisted.

After permanganate was applied to his cut and he was bandaged, we went to an off-license bar next to the Casino Cinema. I knew this place as one for cheap liquor besides being of the type that older men loved because the proprietor did not blare music from juke-boxes. I had visited it about three times before and had found it quite fitting for Dr GG's type. Surrounding it were rooms rented by petty traders and city council cleaners who supplemented their incomes with siesta sessions with Dr GG's age-group. I had a gut feeling Dr Gichinga needed such as a siesta with his booze.

We spent an interesting afternoon during which Dr Gichinga opened his heart to us. Apparently he had quite a stormy marriage with a wife who never appreciated anything he did. He had persevered for twenty years hoping she would change as she grew older. Instead, the lady had become a maniser, terribly gluttonous and avaricious and now she had taught the last two twins whom Dr Gichinga loved dearly, that their father was an evil, wicked murderer with whom they were not to associate. He said that although Kariuki, his brother, had fore-warned him of all these things, he needed to visit his Lavington home to confirm them. I was sorry for him but there was nothing I could do except to make him pick up his surgical skills and hopefully start afresh in life.

We continued having our drinks. I took five White Caps and started feeling slightly drunk. Dr GG ordered what was commonly called a half Vodka for Dr Gichinga and I noticed it was the 350 cubic-centilitre bottle. He (Dr GG) drank Tusker together with Dr Gichinga's brother who appeared to imbibe the stuff with relish. As we continued drinking a young woman joined us and I noticed Dr Gichinga eyeing her rather lustfully. Dr GG, who knew his employer's habits more than I, encouraged her to sit next to the *"daktari"* and ask for a drink. She asked for a Guiness Stout with Coca-cola and was brought two bottles. We continued drinking and I noticed Dr Gichinga getting extremely excited with the lady whom we learnt was Flora from Uganda. They started conversing in Luganda and this must have brought sweet memories to Dr Gichinga, who had studied years ago at Makerere.

They got very animated and the normally dull, closed in, Dr Gichinga opened up. His stammer became less noticeable.

Flora lived in a corner next to the off-license bar and she invited Dr Gichinga to go and see her lodgings. I smelt danger and, in a whisper, enquired from Dr GG whether I should run to a chemist and bring our friend some Durex condoms. The old man broke into uncontrollable laughter.

"He never touches condoms. All he does is to swallow a handful of antibiotic capsules," Dr GG told me. "In fact let us assist him. A lady for one out of prison is the greatest gift one can give to a friend." I was so naive and had forgotten that in prison, sex was one of those things prisoners yearned for most and that prison inmates were prone to inevitable homosexuality because of sex starvation. We encouraged Dr Gichinga who took Flora to her lodgings. Since the lady was a Ugandan, we knew that he was in good hands, unlike with some local girls who were infamous for stealing from and mistreating clients. Dr Gichinga came back after three hours looking fresh, happy and relaxed.

Dr Gichinga got a job with the Prince Kwan Hospital, one of the leading private hospitals in the city. When I saw him a month after we had collected him from gaol, he appeared composed, clean and calm. He told me he had reclaimed his residence although the wife had disappeared to a farm of theirs in Kitale together with all the household goods. She could keep, the farm he said, until he had executed a plan he wouldn't disclose to me of guaranteeing his rights to his property. I did not bother to find out what the plan was as I knew there were many ways of realising one's goals. He needed cash and was ready to "surrender his rights", as he put it to the River Road Clinic "at a consideration of some fifty thousand shillings". I told him that there was forty in the account that ran the clinic but this belonged to the business, not to either of us individually.

"That is exactly what I am saying," he said, getting quite agitated, "I get my share, which I consider is worth fifty thousand and you continue alone." I was not very good in business but the thought of owning the clinic, to run it as my own, appeared quite attractive.

"All the legal formalities will be made, isn't it?" I asked.

"Of course and the Barclays will also be informed."

Barclays was where we banked our money and I left Dr Gichinga, who understood these things, to deal with them so long as he required no further funds from me and he left, as he said he would, enough funds to run the clinic. Two days later, he returned with the proposal that he would collect twenty thousand shillings then and ten thousand monthly until the full amount of fifty thousand was repaid. In the meantime Barclays had accepted an overdraft of ten thousand shillings for running the clinic, as long as the clinic maintained an account. The collateral for the facility was the furniture, surgical and medical equipment used in the clinic. It sounded an agreeable arrangement but I saw the danger signs of bank loans and overdrafts when service to the low income groups is involved. Mary Nduku, who continued to see me in spite of the Ian Brown episode in his house, was terribly excited about the bank overdraft.

"It will now force you to think of the Jaguar," she challenged. I did not bother to answer. I had began giving up on cheap health care as I found myself being more and more a maverick, prices of medicine soaring and even some essential medical supplies missing.

I met Dr GG a few days after Dr Gichinga had "sold" me the clinic and he told me that Dr Gichinga had not told me the truth. Both River Road Clinic and Nderu Clinic had been struck off the register when he had gone to prison. They were therefore technically illegal establishments. On coming back he had tried to resurrect them but had failed hence the sale. I was, he explained, however eligible for registration if only I could apply for them under different names. I applied and got Sigona Clinic for Dr GG who used my name for the purpose of getting a practicing certificate. As for the River Road Clinic, its name disappeared from the notice board and was simply registered as "Dr Joseph Munguti, MB.Ch.B.,M.Med.; VENEREOLOGIST."

In January, 1984, the board went up on the premises I had occupied for nearly four years and I felt really great. I was, I believed the leading venereologist in the country. There was no venereal disease I had not diagnosed and treated other than one case of a Reiter's condition which I referred to the KCH, only to learn that the patient could not find help. In December of 1984, however, a Chinese puzzle came to the clinic. At first I thought it was a simple case of *lymphogranuloma venereum,* then, on a second visit, the sores that I thought were simple genital herpes had spread all over the body. My patient, who called himself simply Kombo, told me he had tried all sorts of medicines in the Nairobi,

Prince Kwan and even the Mater Misericordiae hospitals without success. A friend had referred him to Dr Joseph Munguti and assured him that he would be cured.

"I am a rich man, young man. Here is twenty thousand shillings. Go and look for any medicine that will get rid of this." I would have protested over such generosity but medicines were lacking and I certainly needed to research and find out the latest medicines against *Treponemona pallidum* and *Herpes zoster*, so I took the large red notes' bundle and promised Mr. Kombo my best attention. He left me, looking far more frail than I had seen in any other syphilis or herpes case. If the famous Nairobi hospitals, had heard about me, I thought and they were now referring difficult cases to me, I Munguti, *mwana wa Kiveti*, (we Kambas, whenever excited, called ourselves sons of our mothers), was going to show them I was the greatest. I would spend, I decided the next two nights in the Kenya Medical Research Library till I had found the latest medicines for Mr. Kombo's condition. If the medicines were not available, I had twenty thousand shillings to "D-H-L" medicine from anywhere in the world as the recently very popular courier system was everyday advertising on TV.

The first day I got no clues to what I was looking for. The Reiter's disease did not fit Mr. Kombo's condition. The following day I came across the November issue of the "*American Medical Journal*" and read:

" A serious dermatological condition follows the genital herpes which resists all known antibiotics. Persistent diarrhoea, coughing and swelling of most lymph nodes accompanies the disease. Since the body is incapable of fighting many common diseases, the patient begins to wither away and eventually dies. It has been named the green monkey disease as the virus causing it is synonymous to the one similarly attacking the green monkeys of Central Africa! Several San Franciscan homosexuals are suffering from it."

I was certain about the symptoms I had seen in Mr. Kombo. What I required was diagnosis with clinical tests and further research on causal factors plus an understanding of Mr. Kombo's background. I went for a drink at the "Dog-Section" Canteen hoping to meet a medic with whom I could share my thoughts. I found Dr Nene and Dr Mwanyumba, old colleagues at the KCH and now lecturing at the university. They confirmed my fears that a new sexually transmitted disease had been diagnosed and was transmitted by a strange virus. It had already killed five persons at the KCH, a Finnish man, two Americans and two Zaireans. Three Kenyans had also been admitted with the disease that week. The disease was highly contagious and was terminal. The men and women were therefore isolated in cages from other patients. Only pain killers and sleeping pills plus Kaolin were being offered to them through a gauze-wire screen as the doctors and nurses could not go near them.

My heart beat faster as I listened to the strange story of the green monkey disease. I could however, not sleep before I had solved Mr. Kombo's problem. I left the canteen and drove to the KCH. I took the lift to Ward 22 where I had been informed the patients were caged then introduced myself to the sister in charge. I wanted to look at the patients for comparative purposes, I explained, after which she took me to a glass walled room where three men slept. I felt such helplessness as I watched the helpless men anxiously looking at us. Then I recognized him - there was no mistaking my patient, Mr. Kombo. He frothed at the mouth, arched his back and appeared in great pain as he coughed repeatedly, a dry cough that was definitely puncturing his lungs. He did not recognise me but I felt extremely guilty as I walked away from the cage.

"The one you were looking at is Major Kombo, Cleansing Superintendent of the Nairobi Garbage Handlers Company Ltd. They brought him yesterday and he is unlikely to survive another day," the sister-in-charge advised and I started warming up in the heart. My guilt started waning as I recalled a battered Luo lady who years ago had come to the River Road Clinic complaining of a sodomist City garbage collection boss. I remembered thinking of going to the police station to report a felony, but declined because my medical profession barred me from doing so. Poor Major Kombo, I rationalised, his maker must have decided to avenge the women he had bestialized.

I went back to my flat an extremely worried man. Major Kombo was certainly dying, from the blackening his body was undergoing. He had given me twenty thousand shillings to purchase the most effective medicine, only to be told that there existed no such medicine. I could not communicate this information to him lest he infected me but probably I could return his money. I decided that I would seek a second opinion before giving up. My first thoughts wherever I had a medical problem were to see Dr GG but this one appeared too novel to trust his clinical knowledge with. All the same I drove as I was used to doing, to Nderu to see Dr GG.

Dr GG knew of the disease all right, he claimed. It was called "slim" and had come from Uganda. Only one witchdoctor from Kitui at a place called Tulia, was said to know its cure. Otherwise there was some soil from Mbale in Uganda that was used for its arrest. Although I did not believe in witch-doctors I decided to go to Tulia to seek Nzeki *mwana wa* Uvoo the renowned medicineman of Ukambani who might assist in my predicament. I planned to travel to Kitui on Friday, but this being a Wednesday I could spend the Thursday researching more on how the Americans were coping with the malady. The Kenya Medical Research Institute (KEMRI) was the best on the latest information, but they too were in the dark on how a disease of the monkeys could have got the American homosexuals then passed to African men who did not practice homosexuality. On the way to KEMRI offices, I passed through Ward 22 once more. The number of the patients had increased to ten but two had died the previous evening — a Finn and Major Kombo. Oh God, I called to the heavens. How could you let him die? Here was a man ready to part with a whole life's savings only to die before I had got his medicine! I felt really low.

* * *

Eunice Maimba visited my flat that night and found me in very low spirits. I told her of how my clinic had now become a dangerous place to practice in, because a contagious disease had sprung up. One of my patients had left me twenty thousand shillings to seek the best medicine and he had died before I helped him. Did she think, I asked her, that I should look for the man's relatives to return the money?

"Don't be naive, Joseph. Use the money for the purpose it was given and save others," she advised. "Looking for relatives is unnecessary and would be against the dead man's wish. By the way I need help. My husband does not appear healthy either. He has started having persistent diarrhoea which is not abating."

"Send him to hospital," I advised.

"He is afraid of going to hospital," she answered.

"Why?"

"The disease you have mentioned Mr. Kombo died of," she said and I noticed she was trying to restrain some tears. "He talked to his doctor who thinks he should have his blood tested and the implication was that the killer disease may have struck him."

"He has to be examined if he expects assistance," I said stubbornly.

"This is what I told him but he became very violent. He said that I wanted him to die so that I could inherit his property and that he was leaving nothing for me and my lover-boy," she began sobbing. "Oh Dr Munguti, what shall I do?"

I tried to comfort her as best as I could. She appeared to have coped with the previous problem of sodomy, I thought, because she was not referring to it and then a more frightening matter flashed in my mind. Suppose the husband actually had contracted the green monkey disease that was known as transmittable through sodomy; Oh God! hell had broken loose with this new plague. The thought of Eunice Maimba looking like Major Kombo, with all that healthy body wasted, made me shudder.

"Oh no!" I screamed aloud.

"What is the matter, Joseph?" she asked.

"Nothing, Mrs. Maimba," I lied.

I advised her to use whatever means to see that her husband was thoroughly examined. He was not only a danger to himself but to the whole family. As for me, I would go to Kitui and have a chat with Nzeki *mwana wa* Uvoo, who may be able to help her husband and the others with similar problems.

I drove to Kitui early on Friday morning, arriving at Tulia at around twelve noon. The witch-doctor's place was well known and I had no difficulties locating it. It was a large compound holding ten huts, all round and equal in size, other than for one main one in the centre which served as the old man's surgery/pharmacy/theatre or whatever medical practice he performed. I explained my problem and wanted him to travel with me to Nairobi. He showed me all sorts of paraphernalia——herbs, charms, cowries, skins, feathers, snake fangs and skeletons out of which he concocted medication for the very complex maladies he handled. He would, however, never go to Nairobi. His patients had to visit Tulia and the theatre we were in, if they expected any help from him.

After the fracas in Ian Brown's house my relationship with Mary Nduku soured to the extent that I no longer enjoyed sleeping with her. Her visits to my new flat at the Milimani, grew less and less and finally stopped altogether. With Mrs. Maimba, things were even worse. The very thought of her herpes zoster made my balls shrivel and bury themselves somewhere inside.

I was feeling lonely and low when the phone rang. It was as if the heavens were answering my sexual prayers.

"Hallo, is that you, Dr Munguti?" It was the unmistakable voice of Dr GG's daughter.

"Yes, how are you lovely princess," I said a bit agitatedly.

"Fine, thank you. I am coming home."

"When?"

"Meet me, tomorrow morning at seven o'clock."

"Where?"

"At the railway station," then she rang off before I could say another word.

I collected her at seven in the morning as instructed. She had three heavy trunks that nearly crushed my boot. She was looking extremely lovely, with strands of artificial hair that fell to her shoulders the way English film stars make theirs fall before joining their lovers in bed, I thought. Her yellow-with-mauve flower dress was also exquisite, making her far more graceful than I had seen her before. She was not smoking I noticed but I did not inquire whether this was temporary or complete withdrawal.

"Are they expecting you?" I asked, thinking of driving her straight to her home in Nderu.

"They, who?" she asked.

"Your parents?"

"I am not going to Nderu yet; and I am extremely tired," she said. I then understood the home she referred to during the previous day's telephone conversation. I drove to my flat, off-loaded her baggage then left her sleeping although I had a deep urge to join her before going to the clinic. Work at the clinic was becoming less and less attractive as we missed various drugs and essential pharmaceuticals. I had understood that many fellow doctors now gave prescriptions and not medicines but when I tried this with my clients, I found it extremely unsatisfactory. Many turned back to say they had not found the drugs, others saw prescriptions as an unnecessary exercise for they could have gone to the pharmacies without coming through me. There was also the group for whom oral medicines were sub-standard compared with intramuscular injections. These days I went to the clinic as a duty. The attraction the occupation held for me when I graduated, received Dr Gichinga's blessings to run the clinic as my own and promised to prove to the world that I was Dr Livingstone, Joseph Munguti Schweitzer for the Kenyan venereal disease sufferers, had waned. Our receptionist, one Kinya also appeared bored. He yawned rather more often and would be seen constantly stretching his arms like one who spent sleepless nights. Irene was the only one who, always clad in her spotless white, went about her business with a lot of energy. All she wanted was for me to make sure the clinic had enough surgical spirit and penicillin vials.

* * *

I was now a member of the unique Kenya Bankers' Club which was patronised by many members of the civil service, the big banks and government corporations. In this club most of the people in the who-is-who in Nairobi converged especially on Thursdays. It had five tennis courts, three squash courts, a sauna and a beautiful swimming pool, which made it a particularly convenient rendezvous for Nairobi's young bureaucrats.

I took Mumbi to the club that chilly July evening and we sat in a corner. Dr Nene joined us and I introduced him to my Mombasa visitor.

"This must be the real one now," Dr Nene teased, reminding me that it was high time I settled down with a wife like all the members of the Bankers' Club.

"When you pass the rule that bachelors must cease ..." I retorted.

"Does he claim he is a bachelor?" Mumbi joined in the discussion.

"Well yes, until now," Dr Nene said without realising what tornado he was starting.

"His last day as a bachelor was yesterday." Dr GG's daughter said simply.

After our evening at the club, we drove to my flat. Mumbi told me she had finally left Mombasa since I had now finished with the medical school. Her body was yearning to prove her womanhood and that is exactly what she had come to my flat for. There were to be no more condoms, pills or Depo-provera for the next six months. I made it clear that I was not ready to marry anyone although I confessed I had a lot of interest in her. As a compromise, however, I agreed I could assist in realising her maternal desire so long as the baby was understood as hers rather than mine. Secretly I harboured the wish to prove my virility with a son before I was forty. A lot of women I knew, would have preferred a baby with a husband, but Mumbi was strange. She accepted the arrangement without any reservations. Somehow I knew, I did not want Mumbi for a wife. I owed it to my mother to marry a Kamba girl and although it was taking rather long, I knew that somehow I would find her in Tala or elsewhere.

I lived with Mumbi throughout July, August and September of 1984, then one morning she woke up and joked that if I did not want her, I should drop her at a bus-stop and somebody else would claim her within an hour.

"I thought people did not want married girls any more?" I joked.

"You have refused to marry me." I noticed she was getting angry and serious.

"I have not," I defended myself.

"Dr Joseph Munguti, it is men who woo women but because I broke the rules and put it in a platter for you, you have lost your desire for me," she challenged, with words that bore some truth.

"No, I haven't," I lied.

"You will have to come to Mombasa," she simply said and, surely, when I returned the following evening, she was gone. She left me a dear Joseph letter that was terribly disturbing:

22 Milimani flats

Dear Joseph,

I have gone to Mombasa carrying your baby boy. If you need him you must arrange to have him delivered in your presence in April, 1985. Otherwise he will be donated to the Finns who love African children.

Ever loving but not yours,
Mumbi.

I remembered I had been told that she was going extremely steady with a Captain of a ship, I believe was the Blackmann I had met nearly five years ago, in Mombasa. Her letter consequently started a disturbance in my system, that consumed me everyday throughout November and the Christmas festivities. When Irene finally left the River Road Clinic and I was forced to close it, I was overcome by a strong desire to see Mumbi and claim my son rather than have him go with Captain Blackmann. Captain Blackmann whom I had seen only once, caused pangs of jealousy in my heart, I realised, more than any other living creature on earth. I would imagine his long legs in the middle of the frail body of Mumbi fully astride and literally shut my eyes even if the flash was simply occurring in my brain. When I imagined her screaming to him as she reached the ecstatic orgasms I was so used to, I would shut my ears, sweat profusely and curse.

In January 1985 I started counting the days to the birth of my son. I argued that if it had occurred in August, then the foetal

148

journey had been half-done. In April or May, I would stop being called the Kenya Bankers' Club casanova as Dr Nene had once labelled me. In February when, I could stand it no longer, I wrote to Mumbi a letter expressing my love for her and my unborn son. I invited her to come to Nairobi in April (it had to be April, I had finally settled on the arithmetic) and we would see to our plans. Even though I still yearned for a Kamba girl to appease my mother, I argued, that right then, there was sweet little Mumbi and a son about to be lost to a Finnish bastard. I just couldn't let that happen. My other lovers had, after-all, become untouchable with Ian Brown not letting Mary Nduku see me if she was to receive financial support and Eunice Maimba carrying herpes zoster.

* * *

The year 1985 was a most trying period of my life. All pharmaceutical items shot up in prices, making our clinic extremely expensive to run. The green monkey disease made things even worse for those of us who catered for the down-trodden in society Reports began emanating that the virus was of extreme complexity being transmitted through blood, cuts, semen, vaginal fluids, anal mucus, saliva, mosquitoes, tears and childbirth. Homosexuals and drug addicts, who shared needles, were in particular extremely prone to the spread of the disease through cracks in the anal walls and blood mixing during intravenous drugs' application. Major Kombo sodomised women, I argued. How then did he get the green monkey disease? Kenya had few if any homosexuals and drug addicts using needles. We as a rule made love to women and smoked marijuana although a few male prostitutes had sprang up for Italian and German men in Malindi and Mombasa. Could this then have been the route of the disease which was reported as spreading like a fire in San Francisco? I puzzled further. If the disease was from the green monkeys of the Congo, how did it find it's way in and transfer to the *Homo sapiens.* Yes, we had monkey handlers even in our Primates Research Station newly opened in Nairobi, I thought but still this   a puzzle best left to the

Pasteurs of the world. In any case, I argued, the World Health Organization had started giving serious thought to the plague.

My immediate problem was my clinic in which every week we were receiving frail, emaciated and more genital sore cases than before. Diarrhoea, persistent coughs and swollen lymph nodes were also getting more frequent forcing me to start wearing a mask and gloves. Irene, in particular, began feeling extremely insecure. Our needles would no longer be shared and she, too, had to use a mask, gloves and a plastic apron. Or must she start using an asbestos coat? I wondered. We could put a notice that all serious venereological problems had to be admitted in KCH, but this would still require our diagnosis before we referred men and women to the hospital.

I came a week after Major Kombo had bequeathed the twenty thousand shillings to me to find a note from Irene:-

Dear Dr Munguti,

    I have left the clinic with a very heavy heart. I have been offered a very attractive job by Canaan Hospice as an anaesthetic assistant and as you know my ambition has been all along to specialise in anaesthetics, I have jumped at the chance.

    I think you should look for other work too. It is now unsafe to specialise in the green monkey malady, for you are too nice to risk your life over it.

I will always love you.
Yours sincerely,
Irene.

I wept heavy tears, I do not know exactly why. Irene was right to leave. I also knew I had to close the clinic. I had sworn on the Hippocratic Oath long ago that the welfare of my patients was to be my utmost concern. I thought of all those people, Mother Teresa, Livingstone, Dr Schweitzer who dined and lived among lepers for the sake of humanity. Here, however, I thought, was a disease that was going to kill me no matter what precautions I took. I decided to visit my home town and stay with my people for a few days to think as no one could now help me.

Canaan Hospice had robbed me of the only dear friend I had in this world. I would see her, I decided, before I left for Tala. I was locking the clinic when Eunice Maimba came driving her BMW. She said she had a very urgent matter to discuss and had to see me straightaway. I asked her to wait while I locked up the clinic as our receptionist had failed to appear that morning.

I entered her car and she drove off without telling me where she was taking me. I noticed she was crying and was extremely restless. She drove off Ngong Road and as we were passing Dagoretti Corner she started her strange story.

"You were right, Dr Munguti, my husband has the green monkey disease," she started.

"How do you know?" I asked.

"His doctor took him to that expensive Nairobi Hospital where he stayed for a week. Although his coughing, diarrhoea and sores have subsided, he was advised to keep off my bed for a while, but hid the instructions from me."

"Then how did you know?"

"You know, since that time, he infected me in the bum area, I have kept my bedroom locked," she continued. "Last night he bashed the door with an axe and I had to escape through the window."

"Oh my God," I could not help swearing.

"Yes, I drove to his doctor who told me that under no circumstances was I to sleep with him for a while; he has the green monkey disease. Oh! Dr Munguti what shall we do?"

"I do not know." Already I was feeling unsafe again. Suppose the husband gave her the green monkey disease also, I thought. Then I remembered what I had last treated her for. I began sweating profusely as I noticed her leave Karen shopping centre and enter the little Inn next to the Karen riding school.

"Eunice, I do not know what we should do. I think right now you should take me back to Nairobi. I need to go to Tala for a few days. A lot has been happening lately and I need a few days to put my thoughts together," I said.

"I could come with you," she volunteered.

"No," I barked. She did not realise that all of a sudden I had become terribly frightened of her. "You must go into hiding also. In the meantime, I will consult a cop who is a close friend over your husband's harassment." She refused to drive me back to Nairobi, so as soon as we entered Karen Inn, I excused myself as if I was going to the urinal, then like a hunted animal, I jumped over the fence and ran for my dear life to the bus-stop.

That night I slept a very worried man and I dreamt that I had made love to Dr GG's daughter after which she had gone to the bathroom. In the bathroom she overstayed and I called after her. She did not reply and when I opened the door to check what she was doing, I found her disintegrating before my eyes, from the beauty she was, into a very thin person, then a skeleton, which started spinning in a boiling pot... then I woke up cursing. The dream appeared so real!

* * *

I visited Canaan Hospice the day following my escape from Karen Inn. A friend had that morning told me that it was the old University Workers' Club, next to the International Casino that had been turned into Canaan Hospice. On reaching it I introduced myself as nurse Irene Kamanja's friend. I was advised that she could not be seen at that time as she was busy in the theatre. I could, the receptionist advised, return around two o'clock. I decided to while away the time at the Kenya Museum which was close by. I started with the snake park where I watched the pythons, crocodiles and the tortoises. So many creatures, the maker had made, I began thinking... the birds, the amphibians, the reptiles, insects, mollusca and the mammals. Did all these suffer from the green monkey disease? I wondered but thought it impossible. The disease must involve only those animals that penetrate each other during intercourse. Then the test-tube reproduction came to mind. Yes, I told my confused mind, test-tube reproduction did not involve penetration and was therefore safe.

I left the snake park remembering the Museum had the whole lot of the mammalian world. They were all there, gorillas, chimpanzees, lions, elephants, zebras, rhesus monkeys. How about the green monkey? I asked the curator and was advised that I could see some at the primates' centre in Ngong.

I drank a Fanta and ate a bun then started walking back to Canaan Hospice. Irene came as soon as she heard I was at the gate. She appeared so resplendent in an extremely white dress, white shoes and even white gloves.

"Dr Munguti how are you?" she began. .

"Sister Irene, I am not fine," I answered.

"What sins have we committed?" she asked.

"Maybe, it is those we haven't that are the cause of all this," I answered and I actually meant it. I had very often thought of Irene as the best of the companions I had, but for some very strange reasons, I could not bring myself to wooing her for anything else other than work, sitting and eating together. Whenever I had a date with Irene I would take her back home then look for either Mary Nduku or Eunice Maimba if I required sexual gratification. To be with Mary Nduku or Eunice Maimba was now risky. Irene was the safest female to associate with, I thought, then listened to what she had to say.

"He is here," she said.

"Who?" I asked.

"Dr Waweru Gichinga, but now a completely reformed man. He is so kind and humane, you cannot connect him with the Ward 20 activities," she said.

"Yes, I thought I noticed a complete metamorphosis the day we got him from prison. And even the time he came to "sell" the River Road Clinic. What is he doing here?"

"He is apparently a partner in this home. Dr Ding-Singh who owned it worked with him at the Prince Kwan Hospital. He asked Dr Gichinga to join him here. By the way, you should come too," she said.

"Why?" I asked.

"The pay is good and a hospice is not like the clinic. There is better protection for clinical work even from the green monkeys," she said then went on to apprise me of the history of Canaan Hospice. It was an impressive story, one that left me wondering who had told it to Irene. She told it with an intelligence and analysis I was not then aware she had.

It was more of a terminal diseases' nursing home than an ordinary hospital. All the ingredients of a hospital were, however, available — a casualty ward, theatre, X-ray, laboratory, maternity, nursery, morgue, everything one could think of in a very modern medical centre. It had 28 beds divided into four wings - the maternity which contained seven beds; the general female wing with eight, six beds for male adults above the age of fifty and a special male ward that admitted men of below fifty years but not younger than sixteen years old. The hospice accepted all medical cases except orthopaedics, paediatrics, psychiatry and optical issues. It, however, specialised in obstetrics, gynaecology, respiratory and dermatological diseases and insisted on those who wanted and could afford the very best, accepting deposits of fifty thousand shillings before one was allowed inside the walls of the hospice.

The food, accommodation, coffins, perfumes, linen, cutlery were all the ultra-modern types comparable to, if not more exquisite than, those found in the Mount Kenya Safari Club. It was manned by four doctors, Ding-Singh, Gichinga, Hugh McDonald and To Ktoon, a Filipino who had since been dismissed on being discovered homosexual. The directors were busy looking for a replacement, Irene informed me and asked me to seriously think of it. In a hospice, she argued, one was safer from infection compared with dispensaries, health clinics or even ordinary nursing homes because hospices had the capacity to cope with any medical eventualities.

A former University Lecturers' Club had been turned into this unique place that Irene handed me over to my old employer for a thorough exposure into. As we moved along seeing the various facilities, I told him of my plans to close down the River Road Clinic.

The green monkey scare had made everyone extremely wary and uncomfortable and I wondered how they coped at Canaan.

"Because of the high costs of services here, we are the ultima. We receive clients who have by and large been handled elsewhere, therefore the cases are well-known before they come. If the issues are terminal as is often the case, we make the necessary arrangements," he said simply.

"What necessary arrangements are there with the new threats?" I asked.

"The masks you see all around, special cages, special body rites, all special things that the dying may require," Dr Gichinga said and I had a gut feeling there were some things he did not want to disclose.

Canaan had been the brainchild of Dr Ding-Singh, a medical pracitioner who had also read some economics. He had seen the big gap between the rich and poor Kenyans, looked at their consumer habits in the Hilton, Serena, Beach Hotels, while their brothers and sisters sipped *busaa* in filthy River Road bars then thought he could sell Giffen goods with a special morgue he called, "The de-luxe final journey services." He found that some people in the city even paid for coffins for as much as a hundred thousand shillings. Although euthanasia was illegal in Kenya there were special cases that were entertained as part of the de-luxe final trip services. After this, followed adoption arrangements and special abortion cases. Dr Ding-Singh was a consultant at the Prince Kwan Hospital which he used a lot for obtaining clients for his special services.

He had met Dr Gichinga in the doctors' mess one afternoon and they had discussed current medical issues on euthanasia, abortion and medical ethics.

"There is this new disease for instance for which there is no cure," Dr Gichinga had observed.

"Yes and the shame the sufferers of it are subjected to," Dr Ding-Singh added.

"They are now confining anyone diagnosed as having it."

"Yes with no medication other than throwing make-believe tablets at them."

"We could lessen their suffering," Dr Ding-Singh told Dr Gichinga and invited him into his Canaan Hospice project. Dr Gichinga learnt that there was nothing new with the rich buying secrecy in private hospitals. He reminded him that when Henry the sixth had syphilis, he was reported as having eaten a pig!

After going through the hospital Dr Gichinga came up with the proposal of having me join the Canaan team. He quoted a monthly salary of twenty thousand shillings with a car and housing provided. I looked at him in disbelief. However, when we later saw his partner, Dr Ding-Singh, who appeared an extremely honest man, I believed him and accepted the offer.

I shut the River Road Clinic the following morning and reported to Canaan Hospice with the only condition that my son would be born there.

"Which son?" Dr Gichinga asked.

"The one in my marrows," I said, remembering I had only a month to go before I got a son and wedded Dr GG's daughter. My meeting with Irene that afternoon, however, disturbed me. I had so often left her for other women and all the time she would watch nonchalantly, never letting me know if she approved or not. Secretly, I knew I wished to know her real feelings towards me.

Two days after starting work in Canaan, I began feeling like a captain who had fled a capsizing ship before his crew had abandoned it. I promised myself that I would continue with my campaign for cheaper medical care as far as VD was concerned as soon as the monkey disease patients' management was sorted out and medical supplies became readily available. In the meantime, the River Road Clinic would remain closed and I would hibernate away from it and its risks in Canaan Hospice where the problem was to provide the very best for men and women of Major Kombo's type, those capable of paying for medical care of whatever cost. The contrast between the clientele of the River Road Clinic and Canaan was exciting to observe particularly in their general demeanor, freedom in discussing their condition(s) and the absence of financial worries on the part of the Canaan people. Generally Canaan clients were terribly concerned with their health believing that money could conquer all maladies. I was put in charge of my specialty, venereology and was soon surprised by the prevalence of sexually transmitted diseases among the upper echelons of society as those that patronised Canaan. I had believed that access to better sanitary conditions would make the situation better for these people but I observed that, *chlamydia, trichomonas, herpes* and *gonorrhoea* attacked these people as frequently and as much as it did the River Road Clinic patrons. My job was to research on the latest medical advances on the diseases and handle them in the best way possible. Economy was subordinate to speed and it did not matter whether the drugs were available in the country or not. What mattered was the drug identification and matching with the problem at hand. Canaan, rightly or wrongly, developed over the years it existed into a place where the clientele believed that so long as they could afford, all medical issues were solvable. The receptionist, while accepting the deposits, however, made sure that optical, psychiatric and things connected with orthopaedics were referred elsewhere. When I asked Dr Ding-Singh why the exception, he merely shrugged his shoulders and told me that every medical man had his dislikes and these he had long discovered were branches of medicine he did not like.

"Dr Munguti, you chose to specialise in diseases below the line. It is for similar reasons that Canaan chose to exclude the eyes, the brain and the skeleton out of its occupations. You better concentrate and learn all there is to know about sexually transmitted diseases. I expect in particular you to sort out this monkey disease Chinese puzzle," he admonished, then went on with a favourite subject, "medical ethics." I discovered that he was extremely well versed in the subject. He talked of the controversies generated by euthanasia, test-tube babies, abortion, adoption, infanticide, blood transfusion, heart and kidney transplants, brains' verses, hearts' determined deaths and many problems that faced medicine-men all over the world. He had travelled widely picking up bits and pieces of newspaper cuttings on medical issues, legal reports particularly in the courts of America and Western Europe. He bound them into a large folder file which he gave me to study. From it I read about a famous legal tussle involving a brother and sister who sought for and were granted permission to wed, against the wishes of everyone including their parents. There was the American girl's struggle for a "right to die," where parents sought for years to free their loved child from a life machine she was strapped on for two years. A case that interested me most, I presume because of my pre-occupation with venereology was one where a white faithful wife brought forth a black baby. Many theories in human genetics were proposed but they all failed in sorting out the problem. The puzzle was, however, finally solved with the discovery of a neighbouring house's prostitute out of whom the husband had fished out with the prepuce, a black man's sperm. We discussed the Kenyan laws with regard to medical practice and Dr Ding-Singh was fairly conciliatory.

"Kenya will accept euthanasia, abortion and suicide when the country is fully developed and ceases to enter the band-wagon of English law-makers on all issues. Can you imagine the country's witch-doctors, herbalists, quacks and charlatans being given a free choice on these things?" he asked.

"It can result in a fair mess," I agreed with him.

"Mark you, the courts are silent on those things that are harmless like teenage pregnancies being terminated, lessening the suffering of those in death's way and we have saved many mongoloid and similarly handicapped infants from the cruel fangs of this world," he summed up, ending by warning me of many problems he foresaw with the green monkey disease. "Your area now involves a terminal disease that people are made by society to feel more ashamed of than scrotal elephantiasis. It also involves, I learnt recently, mother-to-child transmission. You had better be prepared, Dr Joseph Munguti. Canaan expects a lot from you," he warned.

Every other day, our daily newspapers the *Citizen*, the *Yardstick* and the *City Times*, ran stories about the monkey disease. I followed these with a lot of interest. A particularly contentious issue was the origin of the disease. The western media claimed it came from Central Africa from the green monkey, *Cercopithecus aethiops sabacus*. African countries were immediately up in arms against this theory and produced evidence of lack of homosexuality in most of their people. Then the Russians brought in the theory that genetic engineering by the Americans who wanted to use the disease for biological warfare, was the cause of the disease.

I spent many hours reading particularly reports by the USA National Cancer Institute. It had published a comprehensive report on the Human T cell Lympotropic Virus type III (HTLV III). In Paris the Pasteur Institute had isolated the green monkey virus from an individual with enlarged lymph nodes and called it Lymphadenopathy Associated Virus (LAV). In about three months of stay at the Canaan, I had become the watchdog for the green monkey disease to whom everyone was sent before being admitted to the hospice. I was back to square one; back to the masks and gloves of the River Road Clinic where millions streamed hoping I had an answer to the HTLV III.

* * *

Mumbi arrived at Canaan on March 15th, 1985. She had come as a patient and not as my girlfriend she told me. When she was brought to my examination room and went through the necessary screening for HTLV III, I explained to Dr Gichinga that the baby I had talked about as a condition for my joining the Canaan had finally been brought for delivery. I also mentioned that she was Dr GG's daughter. She surprised us, however, by insisting that she pays for her medical expenses and that she required no preference as far as these (fees) were concerned. However, Dr Gichinga prevailed upon her to accept the Canaan's generosity on account of her father, Dr GG, who had taught him and many others the art of looking after the sick. Mumbi was free of the diarrhoea, herpes zoster, dermatological disorders and high fever associated with the green monkey disease and received a bed at no cost to her because she was carrying Dr Munguti's son.

A day after her arrival, at the Canaan, a white man was brought to my examination room. He was tall but bent double because of severe abdominal pains. Dr Ding-Singh explained that the authorities had turned the patient back at the airport. It appeared no airline wanted him because they suspected he had contracted the killer disease. I was required to contradict these views and issue him with a certificate indicating his malady was different. This would enable him to go to England, his mother country, to seek medical help there. I could not believe that Dr Ding-Singh was asking me to falsify information for the convenience of an individual. I flatly refused to be party to such an arrangement.

"Dr Munguti, the world does not as yet have the facts about the green monkey disease. Today they have reported that it is no longer a homosexual matter but is even prevalent among us heterosexuals. What falsehood is there where truth is unknown?"

I examined my patient, whom they called Bob Smith. He appeared extremely familiar. His cheekbones protruded and he had lost nearly a third of his weight. The ribs, femurs, pubic bones and even the thigh bones all appeared as if they were separating from the flesh. He had been treated for his cough at the Nairobi Hospital without success and now the diarrhoea attack was eating into his bowels. I had no doubts about what had assailed the white man and I told him he had the green monkey disease. He said he had suspected this but required to go to England for treatment for which he was capable of paying millions. I suggested that if normal passenger planes had declined taking him, he could charter a jet. But there was no jet-flier willing to share a journey with him either.

I did not see why I should falsify my results. It would have earned Canaan a hundred thousand shillings, but Dr Munguti was not going to be party to an arrangement that could easily hasten the spread of the monkey disease, I swore. I had long ago watched a film *"Cassandra Crossing"* and known the dangers of contagious diseases within the confines of public transport. I explained these dangers and my misgivings to doctors Gichinga and Ding-Singh, who threatened me with a sack. The following day the story was in all the newspapers, of a monkey disease sufferer who was refused treatment at the Canaan Hospice and shot himself inside his Mercedes Benz. The police had since released his name as Ian Brown of Sheffield, England.

I mourned Ian Brown but felt no remorse. I had more problems in my hands than I had bargained for when I got a twenty-thousand salary job at the Canaan. Dr McDonald had delivered a baby who proved to be suffering from the green monkey disease. The mother was going to commit infanticide if she was informed of the condition, yet the hospital could not leave it with other children in the nursery for fear it would infect them. As the man in charge of these cases I had to advise on the best options. Dr Ding-Singh contemplated euthanasia for it, but I protested, arguing that my *Hippocratic oath* was against it. As of the prophetic statement that it never rains but pours, Dr Gichinga brought me the news that I had a healthy baby boy, but he was white. Oh God! I had to flee Canaan to bury my head in the sand with shame. My Finnish friend, I then knew, had gone before me in the race for a baby boy with Mumbi, Dr GG's daughter. I could neither face her nor the baby and after her two days' post-natal stay at the Canaan, Irene came to my office with the news that she had left, gone straight to the airport and boarded a British Airways plane bound for a European destination. Tears welled in my eyes but I suppressed the urge to let them flow. Irene understood my anguish and left me with our endearment code of "poor Dr Munguti," to which I answered, "c'est la vie," and locked my door behind her.

The next day the *Yardstick* covered in detail the story of a tycoon, one Godfrey Maimba, who had withdrawn two hundred thousand shillings from the bank, spent a fraction of it with prostitutes in Nyeri town, only to be discovered he was suffering from the green monkey disease. He was arrested, but as there was no law prohibiting a man from having a good time with his money, he had been released. A week later, Eunice Maimba came to the Canaan and told me she had to flee the country because her husband was out to infect her with the green monkey virus before he died. I felt that there was no escape. All over the country the plague appeared to threaten everyone. In Meru, a dashing angel of the town, was reported to have contracted the disease yet she had slept with all the town's bureaucrats. The administration officers sang in unison for her blood, but nothing could be done. Our law had not as yet made the green monkey disease a reportable one and even if it did, one could not be charged with failure to seek medical attention as there existed no medicine for it. The government at the time did not recognise the existence of the plague although evidence was slowly creeping in to show that we were at great risk in spite of the low incidence of homosexuality and intravenous drug abuse in our society.

By 1986, the mode of spread of the green monkey disease was fairly well understood as spread through blood, semen and body fluids. Sex with infected persons whether homosexual or heterosexual was found to explain the prevalence of the disease in Africa. Prostitution was consequently considered a major contributing factor to the spread among the Kenyan population. This threatened our tourist trade and made the government fairly wary of the disclosures about the disease which was by then given the name Acquired Immune Deficiency Syndrome (AIDS). The virus was also renamed Human Immune-deficiency Virus HIV. Studies carried out among the Pumwani area prostitutes revealed that most of them had the virus although they did not show AIDS symptoms. This consequently marked them as an extremely risky group to associate with. Early in the year some British soldiers carrying out their annual military practice in Kenya received instructions to keep off Kenyan prostitutes, an instruction that further infuriated the Kenyan authorities. In the meantime, China and India was requiring AIDS tests for foreign and African migrants in particular. This gave the disease a racial connotation. Demand for AIDS tests by students going overseas particularly to India and China, rose and half of my time at Canaan was spent taking blood samples for reference to the KCH for HIV screening.

Dr Ding-Singh made a trip to London and New York to study how they were coping with the disease. He returned with the idea that Canaan would assist in the fight against AIDS by providing Canaanite certificates to all, particularly Nairobi prostitutes, who were free from AIDS. He also brought along with him an Elisa machine with its kits; recruited a laboratory technician, one Navin Patel and installed it next to my office. I am not sure how the word spread that a certificate bearing the name "Dr Joseph Munguti MB.Ch.B., M.Med.", was an extremely vital document for the country's vice houses. Those men and women who managed prostitution made daily pilgrims to Canaan in search of the Canaanite certificate. Initially the cost for the tests was five hundred shillings. Dr Ding-Singh raised it to one thousand in February, then in March to two thousand. However, in April when he came with the wild proposal that the certificates cost ten thousand, my old phobia for medicine men exploiting the common folk attacked me once more.

"Dr Ding-Singh you cannot do that!" I protested.

"Dr Munguti, you are a hopeless businessman. It is not Ding-Singh who is raising the prices but that fellow Adam Smith called *the Invisible Hand*." Who is Ding-Singh to act against the Nairobi Hilton prostitutes' wishes?" he asked.

"I did not know we have prostitutes operating at the Hilton." I protested.

"Nairobi prostitutes operate everywhere. In the Hilton Health Club, The Big Five of the Inter-Continental, the Serena, International Casino, Panafric, Six Eighty, Florida 2000, Sombrero, Cowboy Arms, the whole bloody city is swarming with prostitutes who need the Canaanite certificates for their trade!" he said, raising his voice at me and I noticed then that he had been drinking. "In fact, I intend to advertise these certificates, but my only problem is that I don't know how to circumvent the KMA's regulations over health certificates. I'll find a way though," he promised.

I found myself shaking with fright at what Dr Ding-Singh was mixing me up with. I saw him completely breaking the rules of medicine and trading in health certificates required by prostitutes and their clients. "Oh God", I cried to the heavens. "How did I get myself into all this?".

As a rule we never conducted tests instigated by the subject directly. It was either through agencies, doctors or clubs. Our mode of advice on the results was simply "negative seropositive" or simply "requiring further investigations." I was therefore safe from the traumas people experienced when told they had HIV - II seropositive results. One day in May, however, a beautiful looking Indian lady clad in a silk sari and exposing her shapely belly, came to the clinic. She asked to see Navin Patel with whom they conversed at length in Hindi. I heard the sound of tables banging but could not understand what Navin Patel and the lady said in their heated argument. The laboratory was next to my office and I walked in to find out what the fracas was about. The lady, who was taller than Navin held a piece of paper before him and demanded to know what the laboratory tests indicated. Navin had strict instructions not to communicate with medical tests' subjects and therefore had refused to answer to her queries. I explained that I was the venereologist and that from her blood we had isolated the HIV virus that causes AIDS. This did not mean she was going to have fully blown AIDS as she could merely carry the virus without necessarily succumbing to it. The lady did not want to hear any more. She cursed, banged the door and ran out of the Canaan. Two minutes later we heard a loud explosion outside the gate then saw a bonfire eating her blue Mercedes. Canaan had started executing people with its disclosures of the killer disease and I was in the middle of the executions. I got terribly worried about my future with the hospice.

* * *

One morning I woke up with swollen salivary glands. I thought these were normal swellings resulting from the large pimples my beard-shaving had caused. The neck was, however, unusually stiff and uncomfortable. I felt below the ears for the parotids and found them swollen, then moved my hand to the sub-lingual and found them diseased. In fright I tapped the sub-maxillary, swallowed saliva and confirmed my fears that all was not well with me. I could not eat the breakfast my cook brought me and I began wondering whether the dreaded disease that had been stalking me for the last ten years had finally caught up with me. Was it with Mary Nduku via Ian Brown? I asked myself, or was it Eunice Maimba through Godfrey Maimba? I sent a prayer to the heavens, then continued wondering if Mumbi, Dr GG's daughter, could also have been the cause of my problem. She had mothered a healthy child all right but this did not necessarily free her from seropositivity, or did it? I continued to ponder.

Captain Blackmann was a Finnish sailor who frequented Mombasa whore houses, so did Major Oluoch, Mumbi's other associate. All this substraction and addition led to the fact that I was surrounded in the last ten years by likely pathways of the killer virus and there was to be no escape. I had coitus severally with the three women, who had done the same with three and more men who in turn had themselves been involved with others. I saw the picture similar to that of a spider-web that traps any flies that come into it and I knew we were all in the web. A sudden fear gripped me as I saw my mother listening to the news of her dear son's final journey and its cause. I saw my clients reading of their doctor who knew all about venereal diseases but could not save himself from them. They were going to mock me as they did Jesus on the cross saying "he saved others, himself he cannot." Was the God I had heard of still a God of love? I wondered. I, who had dedicated myself fully to the service of my down-trodden countrymen and cured them of all those VDs was soon to be reduced into a stinking cadaver incapable of knowing what had made it lifeless. "Jesus be reasonable!" I heard myself shouting then jumped out of my sofa, checked if I could walk, dial the telephone, then speak. I found I could do all that and therefore was still alive. I rang Canaan and told Dr Gichinga I was having a stomach upset and could not leave my flat. He knew I was not a truant and could, he told me, stand for me in issuing the Canaanite certificates that were occupying the whole of the hospital staff by then.

"They have come from Kisumu, Nyeri, Embu, Nakuru, Eldoret, Kakamega, Voi and even Wundanyi and we are even receiving international orders from Uganda and Tanzania," he told me but I did not want to hear of the god-forsaken certificates. I then rang Dr Edward Kimani with whom I had studied in Tala. I wanted a man who still remembered his Hippocratic oath particularly where confidentiality was involved. I knew that if any man could stay honest and faithful to that oath, it was Dr Kimani and I was going to trust my life and pride in his hands.

"Hey, Joseph, long time no see," he still had that charming voice. "How are you?" he continued.

"Can I come and see you straightaway," I said, avoiding to lie in the normal manner in greetings that I was all right.

"Yes, you know where we are?"

"Ya, I'll be there in ten minutes," I answered, then rang off. I entered the new Mazda 625 that Canaan had recently acquired for me and was surprised that I could still drive quite comfortably. Apparently my only problem was in the neck. I parked the car on a yellow-line, not caring if traffic wardens caught me or not, then walked up the three stairs into Dr Kimani's surgery. It was, I noticed, beautifully furnished and carpeted as befitted the upper-class clinics. A secretary-cum-receptionist sat behind a typewriter giving the place a more business-like atmosphere than befitted a medical centre, I thought, then began wondering how long I would carry the cross against medicine-business.

"I have to see Dr Kimani straightaway. I am Dr Joseph Munguti," I said.

"Please sit down. He is expecting you," the beautiful receptionist answered, looking piteously at my swollen neck. A patient walked out of Dr Kimani's office and I walked in. He welcomed me warmly then went on to hug me.

"Please don't come too close and wear your surgical gloves and mask ..." I started.

"Why?"

"I think I have got it and I pointed at my neck."

"Yes you have mumps."

"No, I think it is the killer disease," I said, making him burst out with laughter.

"Whatever has given you those thoughts?" Dr Kimani asked, letting me sit down and going on to examine me without the surgical protection I had urged him to get. He asked me to remove my coat and shirt, lie on the examination couch then proceeded with the routine examination we doctors performed often. He felt the heartbeat, checked my temperature, sat me up and placed the blood-pressure band across my arm. He checked my reflexes with the patellar hammer. He asked me to open my mouth after which he examined it thoroughly using his pencil torch.

"I cannot swallow even my saliva," I told him.

"You'll be all right in no time," he said simply, then went on to write out a prescription. After handing me the paper I asked him in disbelief if he was certain I would get better. He laughed, assuring me that my problem was a simple inflammation of the salivary glands and nothing more. I thanked him and left, bought the medicine in the chemist shop on the ground floor, then drove off back to my flat.

Muya, my cook, had prepared a dish of *ugali* and *sukuma wiki*, that I could not eat. I recalled that some packed instant soups of different types existed in the super markets and these could sort out my feeding problems until I got well (if I did, as I still doubted Dr Kimani's assurances). I fed on the soups for four days, surprised every morning I woke up, that the capsules I had been prescribed, were working. On the fourth day the neck-ache was gone. I thanked my maker and hoped he did not require me in heaven or hell yet.

* * *

I got back to work at the Canaan on a Tuesday, having been away for five days. I found that Dr Gichinga and his associate Dr Ding-Singh had got completely mad with schemes on the Canaan. They were not awaiting or clinical tests any more if anyone paid the required sum of ten thousand shillings for a Canaanite certificate. Dr Ding-Singh argued that reports indicated that the incubation period for the HIV - II virus could be as long as 5, 10 or even 20 years. Absence of it was therefore a meaningless indication since the virus could be developing in the victims' bodies. All there was then, was to cash in on the killer disease so long as people were so scared as to want a useless certificate purporting that they were free from infection. Dr Ding-Singh argued that only virgins who had not got it from their mothers (and very few existed in Kenya), were free of the menace.

"We have bought the house next door for those with full blown AIDS and require our attention," he added.

"You mean you are going to keep AIDS victims here?" I asked in disbelief.

"Yes, now that contact with the AIDS patients has been proven as safe except in blood transfusions and in other body fluids, we can safely look after them," he argued, making me feel that he was, after all, getting humane.

"But still there is no cure," I insisted.

"There is no cure, but you have heard of old people's homes or hospitals for the terminally sick."

"Yes I have. It is high time Kenya had some," I agreed with him, feeling sorry that I had mistaken him for putting money considerations before his obligations to the sick.

"There are people willing to pay fortunes for spending their last days as kings and queens. We shall make them feel exactly that, at a cost of a quarter of a million shillings, of course," I heard and nearly hit the roof in astonishment. "The men will pay ten thousand for quickies, with special condoms provided for them and the women. We've bought Canaan women condoms too," he added. I could not believe what I heard. My employer, Dr Ding-Singh, was, no doubt, insane.

"You make the terminally sick pay for sex?" I asked in disbelief.

"Oh yes, they have no use for the millions in the banks they will leave behind and in any case we'll be providing something they are currently being denied, sex." These men had to be stopped before they went too far.

"I thought Canaan was a respectable hospice, not a bordello," I said with disgust.

"It is a very special hospital, giving the best to the terminally sick."

"And exploiting them."

"Oh! who is not exploiting people through AIDS? The rubber manufacturers of America are making billions out of condoms, blood banks are soaring with business. Writers and film-makers are busy making hay when the sun shines with the AIDS scare. We must hurry, Dr Munguti. We could make millions and each retire comfortably by the time they discover the cure," he said. I found further argument with him useless.

I went to seek Irene at the maternity ward. I had seen very little of her since coming to Canaan but felt I needed her more than I had ever done before.

"Can we meet after work?" I implored her to cancel everything else.

"Any time and you know that, Dr Munguti," she, as usual assured me.

I took her to the Kenya Bankers' Club and we had the usual White Caps (for me) and Pilsners (for her). I explained to her that I felt like quitting the Canaan because of what it had become, a place run by mad doctors who were fleecing the rich with the AIDS scare.

"And where will you go, Dr Munguti?"

"I don't know."

"You should go when you know," she advised and I had to agree with her because very few places paid doctors twenty thousand shillings, gave them cars and took care of the terminally ill.

"Nairobi is becoming a crazy place where making money is involved," I protested.

"Do you know of places with money-making sanity?"

"There must be some. China, U.S.S.R. ... ..."

"Are you sure? In any case, those are not in Kenya," she said and I had to agree with her that there was no escape. Not yet, anyway.

We finished our drinks around ten and it was time to take Irene home. I wondered if I should ask her to go with me to my flat but decided against it. Although I had escaped the salivary glands inflammation, I could not bring myself to risk sleeping with Irene and giving her the virus. It had been argued that condoms could offer protection and Dr Ding-Singh intended vending quickies using them (condoms). But there was a possibility of bursting, besides I could not use condoms on Irene.

"They have started advocating condoms as safe sex now," I started the subject.

"They brought the Canaanite condoms today," she said.

"What?"

"Dr Ding-Singh will leave no stones unturned to make his millions. You and I are supposed to teach Canaan inmates how to use them."

"Oh God," I cried in despair.

"She (God) did not seem to hear," Irene blasphemed, after which I took her to her home, the comfortable bedsitter in the Parklands shopping centre.

* * *

I am not sure how our dailies came to know what was happening at Canaan. Within a week of the creation of the Canaan AIDS Care Centre and marketing of Canaan condoms, all the papers published scathing reports about us.

CANAAN: PROMISED LAND OR WHOREHOUSE; the *Yardstick* headed its front page;

QUARTER OF A MILLION FOR DEATH RITES; the *Citizen* splashed on page one and;

CANAAN, HEAVEN OR HELL? asked the *City Times*.

The stories were similar in theme and approach:

a)   <u>BY YARDSTICK REPORTER:</u>
The prestigious hospice known as Canaan in Westlands is reported as being involved in an unprecedented scandal involving the vending of whoring favours to the terminally sick at the price of all their savings. Started as a funeral directorship for the very rich who required special attention to their dead bodies whether for themselves,

172

relatives or friends, Canaan became the AIDS centre for Nairobi where the first private hospital's AIDS virus isolation machine was first installed. This followed a unique facility of testing for AIDS and granting health certificates known as Canaanite certificates. These certificates, issued to Nairobi men and women, particularly the prostitutes patronising the big hotels, became extremely popular as licenses for sex vending. These licenses, costing as much as ten thousand shillings, have even been exported to neighbouring countries. Of late, Canaan has moved from mere certification on AIDS to management of AIDS patients a noble activity other than for the Canaan condoms introduced lately for the purpose of providing the sufferers (male and female) with sex favours with prostitution. Girls, boys, men and women are being recruited from Majengo Pumwani, Mathare Valley and even Kawangware and "sold" to the AIDS victims with the assurance that the Canaanite condoms will protect them from the killer disease. At the price of between five thousand and ten thousand a night, there are many Majengo prostitutes willing to volunteer.

The Canaan Hospice is owned by Dr Ding-Singh and Dr Waweru Gichinga, both former jailbirds for fraudulent activities connected with the KCH. They have employed two famous Kenyan doctors, Dr Hugh McDonald, a prominent obstetrician and Dr Joseph Munguti. The presence of Dr Joseph Munguti in the Canaan Hospice is a bit of an enigma considering this was the doctor who has for years pioneered against profiteering by doctors in medical practice.

I read the above report and felt extremely low. I could not report to Canaan that morning but had to seek an escape route. Before doing so, I opened the City Times. The three of us were there, God knows from where they had collected our photographs, I thought and read as follows:

b)   <u>BY CITY TIMES REPORTER:</u>
The Ministry of Health must bear the blame for having left such an important exercise to private organizations. By refusing to acknowledge the existence of the killer disease and not attempting to

offer sensible management for the patients the Ministry has allowed unscrupulous men and women to toy with human lives. The Canaan certificates they have vended are like licenses to rabid dogs to go about biting people.

It is understood that not less than fifty men and women have been carelessly informed of being carriers of the deadly disease leading them to either commit suicide or accept the crazy hospitality of Canaan. The hospice has engaged in all sorts and manner of illegality including sodomy, dope-peddling and prostitution of the most bizarre form. The women and men who are paid handsomely for participation in these activities leave the Canaan Hospice most likely diseased adding more to the lepers with AIDS, piling in the country.

Dr Munguti a member of the Canaan team, is the prominent River Road Clinic doctor, who spearheaded for years cheap medicine for the down-trodden members of the society. His ganging up with the crooks of Canaan is a most baffling affair making one feel, wolves can walk in sheep's clothing even in the medical profession. Dr Ding-Singh, who started it all, is a notorious international criminal peddling bang, dope and now vice condoms. His partner, Dr Waweru Gichinga, is a fraud having served several years in the Kamiti Prison for fraudulent activities at the KCH. The Ministry of Health must wake up to its responsibilities and save the nation.

I did not know Dr Ding-Singh had been a world famous criminal although I had not bothered to find out about his past. Two national newspapers had, however, claimed he had a past and I dared not question this. I proceeded to read the last report:

c) <u>BY JOHN KIMARU, CITIZEN REPORTER:</u>
It is now ten years since the coffee boom nearly crippled our economy with a few cashing in on the law enforcement laxity and selling Ugandan coffee as Kenyan. A similar madness has come with sale of Canaan certificates for prostitution to claim freedom from the killer disease. Canaan condoms, claimed as an AIDS cure and advertised with impunity, are some of the deadliest hoaxes to hit the killer-disease world. The perpetrators of the lies of Canaan must be

I had thought of running away but I could not let these people link me with evil things I did not do. I was an employee of the Canaan Hospice and not a party to the things the reports had attributed to it. I had to clear my name through a tete-a-tete with Dr Ding-Singh with whom I had held various discussions on medical ethics and practices as far as the so-called death rites, condoms' vending and sex-bartering were concerned. I drove to the clinic discarding my earlier thoughts of running away to Tala.

* * *

All the government forces must have moved into action immediately the newspapers hit the streets. I arrived at Canaan at eleven to find the NCC in full action demolishing the derelict building that had acted as the AIDS' patients' home. One KCH bus was also around and several police vans, including two of the famous Kenya Police Black *Mariamus*. Besides, there were two NCC ambulances and a contingent of the anti-riot police. One part of me told me I should turn and run away to Tala, the other urged me to join the crowd that had swelled to not less than a thousand people. There were In and Out-patients of Canaan, members of the public that had come to witness action against the scandalous hospital, government and NCC officials that had been asked to see that Canaan ceased to exist. I had done nothing wrong, I argued. I had given the best professional advise on venereology and the little known of the AIDS menace. The Elisa test screening was conducted as far as I was concerned, with all the professional diligence at my disposal. If anyone went outside this and exploited the public, it was not me. I had to have the newspapers receive my side of the story.

I saw Irene boarding one of the NCC ambulances and shouted.
"Irene, please, wait."

"Dr Munguti, run," she screamed. I parked my car, left it hurriedly without bothering to lock it, then joined Irene in the ambulance.

"Where are you going?" I asked, noticing about ten of Canaan patients inside the ambulance.

"They have been looking for all of you since six o'clock this morning. Neither Dr Ding-Singh nor Dr Gichinga has been around. The police only took Dr Hugh McDonald with them around nine o'clock and have been asking for you."

"What do they want?"

"According to Paul Wekesa, you are all members of a vice-ring that has managed Canaan with all crimes reported in the newspapers.

"And what are you doing with these people?"

"We are evacuating all the patients to the KCH as the NCC intends to level Canaan to the ground. Apparently the buildings it has occupied were condemned years ago."

"And the furniture, equipment and hospital records?" I asked in disbelief.

"Only the morgue is licensed, otherwise everything else being illegal, will have to go."

"Did you see the papers this morning?"

"Yes, I did."

"One of the reporters is John Kimaru."

"Oh yes, I forgot, he left Kitale six years ago a terribly battered man. He lost all the shillings he had made in the coffee trade and was reported as having turned to *changaa* brewing in the Karura caves. He could be the one."

"Please look for him in the *Citizen's* headquarters and tell him I would like to see him as he could be useful. In the meantime, I'll turn myself in to Paul Wekesa as I have, I believe, done nothing wrong."

"I know. You are so nice," she said giving me the mollifying cue we had for so long shared.

"You, too. I think it's a high time we stopped being nice," I said, half of which I meant. It appeared as if any time I did something good, someone found fault with it. They were now associating me with the things I had disagreed with Dr Ding-Singh and Dr Gichinga over, the exploitation of patients (however rich they were).

I went straight to my office and found an authoritative NCC inspector taking charge of removing my office furniture.

"Hallo," I greeted him. "I am Dr Joseph Munguti." It was as if I had said I was the grim ripper. The two men holding my cabinet, let it drop and stood like mannequins looking at me, with their mouths agape.

"What?" the inspector let out in disbelief, rolling his eyes and jerking his neck as if to ward off his ears from the blow the mention of Joseph Munguti gave his hearing devices.

"Where is Chief Inspector Paul Wekesa of the Central Police Station?" I asked. I understand he wants to arrest me." I noticed that this further perplexed the occupants of my room who, without answering, left my office one after the other.

"Please don't go," I implored them, " I am not one of the mad doctors they talked about." They did not seem to believe me and when they left my office, they appear to have passed the word like a fire within the walls of Canaan that Dr Joseph Munguti had surfaced. From the window I saw a crowd forming around my room and the people talking agitatedly. I noticed that some of the people who were pulling down the AIDS patients' home joined the new crowd around my office. They carried machetes, axes and three had crow-bars.

"We should smash the building with him inside," one man said.

"No, let's get petrol," another suggested.

"The police require him," a third one protested.

"They said they want them dead or alive," another shouted and I could stand their hatred no more.

"Please, hold it, gentlemen," I protested as I came out of the office. "You can burn me alive if you want, but at least wait until you hear my side of the story."

"Kill the bastard," one evil looking burly fellow shouted.

"No, let's hear what he has to say," a woman shrieked, then I noticed the familiar face of Paul Wekesa. I sent thanksgiving prayers to the heavens because I knew that justice and not emotion would prevail over the Canaan saga.

* * *

Inspector Wekesa took me to the Central Police Station where he explained he was now attached to the criminal investigations branch. The Commissioner of Police himself had directed that he gets to the bottom of the Canaan hospital story, bring all who had wronged the public to book but not let a single innocent person suffer. I made a long statement in which I told him all I knew of Canaan. My lengthy discussions and objections to certain practices, the suicides I knew of, all the deaths and the little I knew about funeral arrangements, the Canaan condoms and certificates and everything I remembered each of us was responsible for. Wekesa was extremely brilliant and saw Canaan from a highly conciliatory angle, as a place that had started with a lot of good intentions, he told me, but one that corruption could not allow to remain clean.

"I am surprised, Dr Munguti, you have remained so incorruptible," he said, shaking my hand and promising to assist where he could.

It took a week to demolish Canaan, store all its equipment, furniture and records in a warehouse at the police station and distribute its thirty-five patients, (who refused to be taken to the KCH), among the three private Nairobi hospitals. Special wings and living conditions had to be arranged in all these that were still reluctant in accepting AIDS sufferers.

Irene and the other nurses were distributed to "herd their flock" (as one of the hospital superintendents remarked) among the three hospitals. As for me, I was too tired to do anything other than pack my travel gear and advise Irene and Inspector Wekesa to get in touch through the Tala Police Station.

On Friday evening at around five, I drove to Tala in the Mazda I had inherited from Dr Ding-Singh, feeling like the prodigal son who was returning home.

I arrived in Tala at around six o'clock that Friday afternoon and drove straight home. My mother who had just returned from the garden, was extremely happy to see me in my Mazda 625, but informed me that our father was unwell and had been admitted to the Tala General Hospital. I did not want much to do with hospitals as yet so I decided not to go and see him that evening. My brother, however, insisted on slaughtering a goat the old man had kept for roasting when I came back to Tala. As they skinned it, I felt like the prodigal son having his father's fattened calf slaughtered. Three of my brothers still lived around the homestead while four sisters were associated with the house, two still living with my mother and two married less than a kilometre from the home. Someone managed to call them with their families to join in the goat-eating, which we started at nine in the evening and ate until well past midnight. We started with the traditional liver and intestines, which had to be passed to every member of the family, then went on to the front legs. After this, each of us had a rib of the delicious meat followed by a piece of one of the hind legs, finishing with the four stomachs.

One of the hind legs was given to our mother for cooking at a later date together with the head and hoofs that were to make soup for subsequent days. At around one o'clock the crowd began dispersing one by one and I found myself finally alone and ready to fall on the bed I had not used for years.

I slept heavily for when I woke up the following Saturday, the sun was up and everyone had disappeared to their daily chores of cultivating in the garden. I went to the kitchen and found that my mother had warmed water for my bath and left a kettle with tea warming by the fire. I washed, drank the tea then drove to Tala town to buy newspapers and listen to the local gossip. Newspapers, as a rule, never arrived in Tala before twelve o'clock and I discovered I had about an hour to wait for them. I decided to walk to the market and see what people vended at that time of the year when food was in short supply. Most of the market contained flour measures of extremely small quantities which sold quite exorbitantly. Apparently Tala had not changed as far as market-pricing was concerned. As a child I had known the months of November and December as times of high food prices. Nothing had changed apparently. A two-kilogramme measure of maize meal was selling for ten shillings, that of sorghum fifteen and finger-millet twenty, I was told. The sources were either Kakamega, many miles away, or from a few farmers around Tala.

I was about to leave the market when I heard a conversation which stopped me in my tracks.

"You remember Yosevu *Mwana wa* Kilonzo, the doctor?" one lady said.

"Yes, the one who went to Tala High School," the other one said.

"He is in town, with a big car."

"Oh! And I hear he is still unmarried."

"Yes, he still hasn't got a wife."

"I wonder what is wrong with him."

"You better send your daughter to find out."

"Why my daughter, I am about his age."

"He will not touch a married woman."

I felt like laughing at the mention of my not touching married women. But I didn't wait to hear anymore. I fled before I either embarrassed myself or the two wondering about my bachelorhood. I bought all the day's newspapers, the *Yardstick*, the *City Times* and the *Citizen* and drove back home where I found my mother preparing *muthokoi* for lunch. The news of Canaan was in the headlines and John Kimaru had ran a beautiful story about me in which he vindicated me fully from the atrocities in Canaan. He reported that Dr Ding-Singh, the devil behind Canaan, as he called him, had escaped out of the country. But there was a sad twist to the whole saga. Dr Gichinga had died in a head-on collision in his Volkswagen near Busia, presumably as he was escaping to a neighbouring country.

We had lunch, which included the hind leg of the goat slaughtered the previous night, its head and four feet plus a mug of soup which my two brothers appeared to enjoy tremendously. After this I drove mother, the two brothers and the youngest sister to the hospital to see our father. He appeared pretty weak but they had diagnosed a malarial attack that was responding well to treatment. I dared not interfere with my medical colleagues over what they were doing because besides knowing he was receiving the best care available in Tala, I could not offer a better alternative as I now had no hospital base. Canaan had been flattened to the ground.

It was the best week of my life. In the comfort of a home I had lived in as a child, with my mother looking after me as if I was a child once more and my brothers and sisters taking turns in making me feel comfortable by accompanying me on visits to our relatives, I shed all the worries that had characterised my life in Canaan. I realised then, that doctoring could cause a lot of mental and physical tiredness because, on the day I entered Tala, all my limbs, neck and back were aching. As the days passed in spite of the walking we did, sometimes amounting to as many as twenty kilometres in a day, the aching eased.

I began wondering why we all ran to Nairobi with its confusion of noise, hustling, shoving, crime, friendlessness, indifference, cheating, high prices, smoke, insecurity and general chaos and left the peace and security of the countryside. A subject I wanted very much to discuss, but found people extremely reluctant to talk about, was the killer disease AIDS. Apparently in spite of the vigorous campaign it had occasioned, my people somehow thought it could not affect them.

"It is in Nairobi, Mombasa and Kisumu," my brother vehemently said. "Tala is free of it."

I dared not contradict him but apparently he had seen some newspaper report of my work in Canaan.

"By the way," he said. "they say you were working with some of these people."

"Yes, I was in a hospital that admitted them."

"How did you feel?" he wondered.

"Well, they are like all other sick people except that some get terribly depressed when they think there is no cure," I said as best as I could. I went on to tell him of the suicides we had witnessed, but avoided the subject of heavy medical fees and the exploitation of the patients Dr Dingh-Singh got the hospital into, but apparently he had heard about this also.

"They said you were killing people," he challenged.

"No, we never killed anyone, but there were a few that got hopelessly sick and had their suffering terminated by their doctors." I knew the concept of euthanasia was too complicated for me to open a debate on.

"How about the women?" he continued. "The women prostitutes who had been paid and brought to Canaan for some eccentric old men seeking a "last bite," as they called it and had been reported extensively by all the papers?" I was not sure how to handle this question without appearing to shift the blame.

"Well, prostitutes have been known to sell their bodies to all sorts of people so long as the price is right. I guess this is what Dr Ding-Singh used as bait for the women. For some of the men, they were ready to have sex at any price because they knew they were dying and had been denied sexual favours by wives, friends and even the prostitutes themselves."

I knew my brother, who had been brought up in Tala in a community where prostitution was unknown and direct payment for sexual favours was unnecessary, would find this difficult to comprehend. However he accepted that the big cities had their own peculiar economic orders into which the rural communities could not fit.

*　*　*

Paul Wekesa visited me on Wednesday afternoon. He must have checked my movements with the local police because he found us drinking at the Tala Inn which we always visited promptly at 5.30 p.m. I was overjoyed to see him not simply because of his honesty and friendliness but because I knew he had the latest information on Canaan. I ordered his favourite drink, Tusker Export, which he took reluctantly reminding me that he was still on duty. I replied that Tala was not Nairobi and that we conducted our affairs with the bottle, outside the city. We took our beers, had some roasted beef, then went on to fill each other in on what had taken place in our separate worlds since parting at the Central Police Station nearly a week before. I told him I had left Nairobi and would not return for a while. I was enjoying myself doing nothing and sampling my mother's cooking. My only worry was for my house-help, who might have starved while I ate so much.

Inspector Wekesa promised to check on him on his return to Nairobi. The investigation on Canaan had now been completed and Dr Hugh McDonald released. The real culprits of the Canaan crimes were doctors Ding-Singh and Gichinga, Wekesa had been able to establish after interrogating the eleven nurses that had worked with Canaan. The government was contemplating tracking Dr Ding-Singh in England where he was reported to have fled to.

As for me, he said, I was wanted back at the KCH where all doctors were now required to offer medical services even if on part-time basis.

"Do I understand you came to hunt for me for the government?" I asked.

"Oh, no, I was merely informing you of what is happening in Nairobi," Wekesa said. "The local police will arrest you if you wish."

I had heard that there had been a shortage of medical staff at the national hospitals because of the dangers AIDS posed but that since the government had established there was no danger in taking care of AIDS patients, doctors were now required to return to work. I explained to Wekesa that I was on leave for a month but would return to serve the nation as soon as it was over. He left Tala around ten in the night promising to see my cook and assure him of my safety.

* * *

On Friday, a week after I had been in Tala, Dr GG and Irene visited us. He seemed older than I had seen him before and far more wrinkled and weak. Irene looked beautiful in a cream dress and a blue scarf plus blue flat shoes to match the scarf. I introduced Dr GG to my mother as a man I had worked with for years and Irene as a very special friend who had worked with me in the River Road Clinic, KCH and, lately Canaan. My mother shook their hands and as she shook Irene's I noticed the special radiance in her eyes that she offered only to people, events or news that she either approved of or appreciated.

"And why have you never brought this wonderful lady to Tala?" my mother challenged.

"I was sparing her to the end," I joked, recalling that she had never approved my bringing Eunice Maimba to her home, even if they had appeared to get along well.

"She must have Tala blood," she went on and I knew that my mother approved Irene like the Tala girls she so much wanted me to have. I did not pursue the subject but took Dr GG to my hut. I detected there was something he was trying to tell me, which was for my ears only.

The news he brought shattered me more than anything I had heard for years. I looked at the grass-roof of my hut and dared not to look down lest I let the tears drop. Mumbi had written to one of her brothers explaining she was having problems in Finland and indicating she was returning. I was to be informed of this but the family had decided against it not wanting to burden me as the Canaan crisis was in full bloom. However, on the day Canaan was destroyed, a cable came from the husband, Mr. Blackmann, explaining that she had died of a mysterious disease and that if the father wanted, two relatives could travel to Helsinki to collect the body. They had enclosed air tickets and assured them that all the expenses would be met by the Captain's family. Dr GG did not know what to do, but had bumped into Irene in the Nairobi Hospital where he had taken clinical test specimens and been informed of my Tala hibernation. Irene had expressed a wish to run away from the AIDS patients at the Nairobi Hospital and Dr GG had offered her a job at Sigona Clinic, but before this could be done, they had to look for me.

I informed my mother I had to return to Nairobi with my friends. She approved, so long as I brought Irene back before long. We left Tala after lunch and drove through my flat, which I had not seen for seven days. I found Muya asleep on the sofa, woke him up and asked him to make us tea while I dressed more warmly for Nderu. He gave me a letter with foreign stamps. I could make out the name **Geneva** on the stamps, although I knew no one in Geneva. Mumbi could, however, have written to me, I thought, as I opened the letter. It was not from Mumbi. The address was of the World Health Organization headquarters in Geneva. The letter said:-

Dear Dr Munguti,
    The World Health Organization has followed with interest the work you have done in Venereology in your country. The WHO would like to interest you in its Global fight against the AIDS menace and wishes to invite you to its headquarters in Geneva for an interview.
    AIDS cases world-wide now estimated at close to 150,000 will double this year partly from the widespread and dangerous belief that nice people are at little risk. All the expenses to and from your country will be paid by the W.H.O. and tickets will be sent as soon as the organization receives a positive reply from you.

Yours sincerely,
Dr Jonathan Mann,
for Director-General,
WORLD HEALTH ORGANIZATION.

I took Dr GG home to Nderu after dropping Irene at her flat. The news of Mumbi's death was too grim for the WHO's offer to excite me that night. Nevertheless I was glad that my labours with the sick at the River Road Clinic were at last being recognized.

EPILOGUE

I told Irene I would have an AIDS Test and she was surprised I hadn't had any. I mentioned that I had no cause to have had one and she laughed, calling me the healer who never dared cure himself. She said that at the Nairobi Hospital they had to have tests. They had initially been told they would undergo simple blood tests only to be informed afterwards of the Elisa test results. Hers was negative.

Dr Edward Kimani took about twenty centilitres of blood out of my left arm, but I had to have him swear over his dead mother's grave that the results would only be known to him and myself. I did not at the time care what they showed after I had seen so many people suffering from the dammed plague. However, when the results, which he relayed on the telephone, came, I could have hit the roof with excitement.

"You are clean, Dr Munguti," he said.

"You mean, so far so good?" I asked

"Yes."

"Thanks to whoever invented the condom."

I could not believe it until he handed me the results signed by none other than Maxwell Hungu of the Nairobi Laboratory Services. It was like giving me a new lease on life, a feeling I wanted to share with only one other person.

I drove to Nderu for Mumbi's funeral and after it was all over I felt a comforting hand holding me from falling. I was blinded by all that crying, but could make out her tall figure.

"I have been offered a job in Geneva, Irene."

"Oh! how good."

"And I am not taking it," I added.

"Why, you stubborn man?"

"I do not want to be away from you."

"You don't have to."

"Can I have Geneva and you?"

"I believe so," she simply said and I knew that all the sojourn with her at the KCH, River Road Clinic, Canaan Hospice and Tala had been leading me to her all along. We left for Geneva on April, 22nd 1987.

BLACK GOLD OF CHEPKUBE BY WAMUGUNDA GETERIA
Published by Heinemann Kenya Limited.

Sometime during the mid 70s a climatic catastrophe in Latin America unleashed a tremendous series of political and economic events whose ripples were to be felt all over the world. Bitter frost destroyed a whole year's crop of the famous, largest-selling Brazilian coffee, and the international coffee market was gripped with an acute scarcity.

Across the Atlantic, in Uganda, the pompous dictator, Idi Amin had led the Pearl of Africa into economic ruin. Agricultural crops could not be easily exported and when they were, the farmers earned very little. The Ugandan Shilling which had previously been at par with the Kenyan Shilling quickly plummeted to the lowest level in value.

While the international coffee market yearned for more of the precious beverage, the Ugandan farmers wished for someone to pay more for their coffee beans. And the Kenyans were more than ready. Thus was born Chepkube.

This is a story of the illegal coffee trade that rocked the border between Kenya and Uganda during the 70s. It is a story of political intrigue, expansive lobbying, instant riches, moral degeneration and death. It is the first ever told story of a people gone mad over the black gold of Chepkube; told by an insider.

> The novel takes the reader through the lives of these individuals, what motivates them to end up in smuggling, the consequences that befell them and the national economy.
>
> The result is a fast reading book that meanders from the dens of vice to the high offices with cosmetic faces and at the end of it all reveals the moral decay that was eating Kenya then.

SUNDAY NATION.

The subsequent illegal dealings, corruption, human greed and envy are the subject of *Black Gold of Chepkube* by a new comer Wamugunda Geteria. He brings this out in a unique freshness and involvement.

SUNDAY TIMES.

Black Gold of Chepkube marks the beginning of a new trend in Kenyan popular literature.

The novel demonstrates that popular literature need not be confined to the role of alienating readers from day to day problems. It can serve a more serious function of warning the society against psychological disintegration.

CIARUNJI CHESAINA
LEEDS UNIVERSITY - UK